Grand Menteur

Grand Menteur
Jean Marc Ah-Sen

BOOKTHUG
DEPARTMENT OF NARRATIVE STUDIES
TORONTO, 2015

SECOND PRINTING

Cover photo and interior photos by the author.

The production of this book was made possible through the generous
assistance of the Canada Council for the Arts and the Ontario Arts Council.
BookThug also acknowledges the support of the Government of Canada
through the Canada Book Fund and the Government of Ontario through
the Ontario Book Publishing Tax Credit and the Ontario Book Fund.

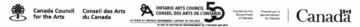

LIBRARY AND ARCHIVES CANADA CATALOGUING IN PUBLICATION

Ah-Sen, Jean Marc, 1987–, author
    Grand menteur / Jean Marc Ah-Sen.

Issued in print and electronic formats.
ISBN 978-1-77166-130-0 (paperback).--ISBN 978-1-77166-131-7 (html).--
ISBN 978-1-77166-132-4 (pdf).--ISBN 978-1-77166-133-1 (mobi kindle)

    I. Title.

PS8601.H2G73 2015   C813'.6   C2015-905699-3
                                            C2015-905700-0

PRINTED IN CANADA

Shelfie

A **bundled** eBook edition is available
with the purchase of this print book.

CLEARLY PRINT YOUR NAME ABOVE IN UPPER CASE

Instructions to claim your eBook edition:
1. Download the Shelfie app for Android or iOS
2. Write your name in **UPPER CASE** above
3. Use the Shelfie app to submit a photo
4. Download your eBook to any device

For Katrina and Chester, my la la la lights of love.

Malbar (left) and Sergent at a Sous function, circa 1963

I.

Rue La Paix, Port Louis, Mauritius, 1956

MY FATHER USED TO RUN around in the mid-forties
with a group of hustling street toughs called the "Sous
Gang." A subject of spirited ridicule, the name was vari-
ously attributed to from as strange a thing as the practice
of sooging catamarans clear of dead fish, to the synchro-
nized smirking members performed when accused of a
crime. One account, brimming with college petulance,
even related the name to the Kreol phrase, "To ene sou
inne vinne cinq sous" (Your penny's become a nickel) – a
veiled reference if anything ever was to distinguishing sod-
omites by their similarity to the dimensions of circulating

coinage. These were young, darned-if-you-did-darned-if-you-didn't children, exulting behind the embrasures of a coconut-studded headquarters, who would arrange themselves for a bizarre allogrooming ritual that spilled out onto the street, the bazaar, or as was often their custom, the Champ de Mars Racecourse. They would blow nits out of each other's heads, and with a wad of chewed gum flattened into a four-inch square, catch the airborne pests, intent on selling them as an ersatz tukmaria for the composition of alouda glace. You will perhaps encounter no more challenging a task than to imagine this farouche network of children, these bandolier-wearing layabouts who carried stale tamarinds clumped into katty quids and were sensible enough to search for ectoparasites among one another, but were otherwise unmindful of honouring society's customs of civility with so much as a grunt of acknowledgment. If a shopkeeper inquired why they were not in school when they walked before his storefront in the noontide sun, they walked on by, paying him no heed, only to return after nightfall to render all of his goods invendible in one manner or another.

The story of how my father came into contact with this network of delinquents is rather a hopeless one. I stress this point because solicitors and constables always believe a lifestyle of crime involves an overdetermination of choice, like you could decide the quality of water that came out of the Colmar Canal into your taps any more than you could decide the colour of your skin. The architecture of survival does not care about those who quibble with its provisions for choice: there is always unfinished business somewhere or other, and an axe to grind can meet life's challenge. Suffice it to say that holed up somewhere in a David Street tannery, poor and left to his own devices, my eight-year-old father would reflect silently on his exclusion, dreaming of the material world.

The Sous Gang meanwhile found relief from Lady Luck's retreating favours in the form of several well-coordinated rackets. It was not known to the majority of the wayfaring public, to cite one memorable example, that in the chiselled-hollow Tin Lizzies abandoned behind a walled junkyard on La Rue Royal, existed an elaborately structured glory hole where two hundred rupees could produce the epiphanic combination of a mastiff's unclenched cheeks and, if one was looking for it, a clear conscience. Though there'd be a greater likelihood of surviving a leap from Montagne des Signaux with a clutch of chickens strapped about your arms than finding true happiness, there was at the very least a sporting chance of getting your money's worth. Their eventual meeting, I have it on my father's word, transpired when the singular circumstance of a vacancy arose within the Sous ranks – a vacancy for a *Grand Menteur*, a position my father knew well from his time panhandling in the street with my grandfather. With his recommendation of a tannin-based tagging system to monitor the diminishing marginal returns of the stray dogs in question, my father was given probationary placement within the gang organization.

By the time he was sixteen, he had already engendered a reputation among Port Louis lowlifes as something of a smooth talker: consorting fellows were wise to avoid his badinage about "the porthole romances of the Silver Tent Gang" or "the blind fortunes of the pushcart poulterer." Such lies soon placed him among thieves and bandits, the tartuffism of their lifestyles enjoining him to forget the old ways of earning money. For there is great reserve in a dependable liar – in somebody one can trust to be tenaciously mistrustful. When asked, "Where's the money?":

Answer: What money?
Question: The money from the horse betting.
Answer: I don't go in for things like that.
Question: You know what I mean.
Answer: The money from the horse betting.
Question: So you admit it.
Answer: I admit to nothing.
Question: You admit that you don't go for things like horse betting.
Answer: I admit I don't go for things insofar as horse betting is involved, yes.
Question: So you don't admit to admitting that you don't go for things?
Answer: You're trying to confuse me.
Question: Answer the question.
Answer: No.
Question: And why not?
Answer: No, I don't admit to admitting I don't go for things.
Question: Then naturally you admit you do go for things; say horse betting, for example.
Answer: I don't admit I don't go for things, generally,

because I do.

Question: Are you some kind of nihilist?

Answer: I don't go in for things like that.

For indeed, all he did was lie; he hardly stole, he trounced no one. His role, like the other Sous before him, was limited to what he exclusively knew best: falling behind the others on the getaway to stall and confab. He handled the police in the same way they handled him – with prejudice and a view toward humiliation. So it was that his encouragement of a friendship with a member of the constabulary, one Malbar, was bound to raise more than just a few eyebrows or, in his particular example, tightly clenched fists.

As far as first meetings go, it fell short of the hope-drawn promises a lifetime of cinematic exposure inevitably bestows. Malbar was an imposing fellow, hunched shoulders and an itinerant jawbone giving him the air of a constipated volcano. He walked with a striding confidence unmatched even in the annals of police history and amazed all manner of peoples with his indifference to those at the mercy of his absurd authority. The brave cock on his dunghill, raised on an unbroken diet of thuggery and snapping hardship, was equal parts bull and insensate, on the receiving end of denigrations only a gazetteer armed with a rotogravure could articulate. The young officer was eager to pass muster, and there posed no better means for this than by policing the stout-hearted brats of the Sous Gang. One morning, in the presence of two lowly gang members,

Declarative: Sa gogotte la enne voleur. Jamais li travail.
Cotte to croire li gagne casse pour li habille coum
ca? Li enne bourrique: li conne ziste coquin, mange,
divertir, caca.
Question: You there, in the red! English?
Answer: Non.
Question: I'm looking for this dog's owner. Er . . .
enough people are complaining.
Answer: Buyer beware, sousoute.
Question: So it's one of you then?
Answer: Mod cons.
Question: Eh?
Answer: Conveniences. We offer all mod cons.
Question: I ought to take you in on charges – charges
of gross indecency!
Answer: The dog is not mine. I have never seen it
before. Ask anyone.
Imperative: Your English has come along considerably
since we started. Leave the strays well alone!
Declarative: Get stuffed!

Malbar followed his instincts home in this fashion, pro-
pelling himself up the chain of miscreants until one day
he found Sergent – as my father was known to others – in
the process of tagging a Sous pup on a deserted thorough-
fare. While another gang member of roughly the same
age (though twice the size) named Ti Pourri held the dog
down, the eager lawman sized my father up with a stinking crook-eye, poised finally for an actual arrest.

Accompanied only by that blear-eyed gargoyle, easily

mistaken for yon young gallant, what with the way he thumped behind like a rudderless ketch, my father simply looked up and muttered to Pourri, "You'll survive," before flying off around the corner to safety. Ti Pourri spent a fine time of it that night surrounded by hardened criminals anxious about the back-door parole, only to be welcomed upon his release with his expulsion from the group. Apparently (the source of which remained flagged in mystery), Ti Pourri succumbed to a statutory ouster on the Sous Charter grounds that he couldn't keep his mouth shut and abandoned his post when faced with the gablou. The seizure of "Old Faithful," as the pooch had been christened among the more reliable of his clients, was in many ways the end of that rather misfortunate use of canine flattery.

Sergent was not ignorant to the benefits of contact with blue arms of the law; such contact kept him spry and reminded him when to be aloof. At times, while cultivating this aspect of being standoffish, he went too far, and even became suspicious of his friend the constable. Meetings with Malbar sometimes sent my father deeper into himself, and the tightlippedness he bore like a badge of distinction grew intolerable. It continued in and out of the home, or so my mother would recount before her sad fate put an end to conversation between us; it must have made some sense, somewhere in the winding cockles of my father's brain, to engage in discourse with a dark concentration that could save him from incrimination. Only my father could conceive the phrase, "You're looking well," as an indictment after all. (How did he look *beforehand*?) Unable to otherwise articulate pleasure, envy, anger, frustration, my father took to his sacred refuge, this vow of unruly silence, with the ardency of the poverty line. But the transition from prolixity to silence did not occur overnight. At first, he began to lose track of stories he'd told certain officers. He squabbled among Sous members over what had allegedly been communicated by his own nefarious tongue. But maybe most significant was that his foundering as the Grand Menteur coincided with the decision that his services were needed by his eleemosynary countrymen. Something in his brain made him realize that even the least deserving were welcome to the ill-gotten gains of his imagination – whether in the form of handing out stolen merchandise, or simply to take the Sous to uncharted ground that would aggravate closed-minded superiors like the infamous Black Derwish, he decided he would become a humanitarian.

"What's this, Sergent?" Malbar asked one morning, wiping the beads of sweat that converged on his nostrils. "You're not out for yourself anymore?"

"I'm the enterprising sort," my father responded.

"Avant ki mo tane rumeur la! I hear that you have convinced the Black Derwish that the police chief is looking for him. That his 'worm-ridden guavas' are somehow responsible for sick officers, and in their absence, escalating crime rates. You have managed to convince the costermonger not only to abandon his fruit, but that both police and those they are responsible for are engaging in one form of backsliding or another. I can assure you, however, that my ability to impede the criminal element remains unwavering – on account of an iron stomach."

"Children of Beau Bassin clinics can say the same."

"You're not capable of charity. You can't have the interests of those children at heart. It's not possible."

Sergent's face remained blank, frustrating his friend's suspicions. By way of appeasement, my father handed Malbar a guava the size of a golf ball.

"When it comes to the subject of suffering children, I can assure you, I am all seriousness."

"How is our good friend Ti Pourri faring these days?"

"Antagonism is not your strong suit. You come evidently to talk, so talk. One of us was born into the wrong profession."

At these words the heavy-framed officer bristled. It was a fact that Malbar had been reluctant to accept. They had kept schtum about their arrangement with most others, allowing them to go about their business, their transactions of exchanged information, with a celebrated facility of movement. The dates for an unscheduled police training exercise could be traded for the location where stolen merchandise was being stored, or perhaps even where a fellow gang member could be nabbed for indecent behaviour; but the balance sheet constantly threatened to spill over into lopsidedness on either side. Malbar dusted off and then quickly replaced whatever reservations stirred within him to their musty place of origin.

"You're right," Malbar said. "It benefits neither of us to continue down this road. Curiosity behoves me to ask you where you've really gotten all this fruit from, if not from the Derwish?"

"You'll not get me to admit to anything. Perhaps as a

matter of pride, but then again, perhaps not."

"Apparently, I have no interest in bringing you to the station."

"Yes. You play your part incredibly well. 'I know nothing about dogs and I know nothing about missing fruit.'"

"'I did not mention dogs.'"

"'Your presumption that I did alarms me.'"

Then followed a moment of grave import, of the first transgression and the first enlightenment, consequences of which are still being felt to this day:

"Tell me, *tournevis*. Are you happy here? Bound by the ocean, these mountains, the peoples' incivility? Bound by the law that I represent?"

"Tsk tsk – you lose. *Partie terminée.* Do not talk to me of happiness if you are not prepared to define it, Malbar. It's elementary."

"The Mauritian preoccupation with it is unseemly," Malbar continued. "More so than other peoples. It is an island pathology."

"Stop hashing potatoes. What do you get at, talking to me about my affairs?"

"There is a whole world beyond the water, Sergent – that's all I meant to imply."

"You remain. Behaving and dressing like me. Correction – *us*. Using our tongues. You wish to discuss pathologies?"

"*Connard*, this is all you know. Are you prepared to live with it being all you have ever known?"

"I have what I need. Mine is a life of practicality: practicality of thought, practicality of action. Maybe you should consider that I do not care to know what is beyond that water."

"Doling out stolen fruit, grinding out a pauper's profit. Guavas and dogs, dogs and guavas. You speak of ambition, but content yourself to run exchange-marathons with canaille and degenerates. You will learn that light suppers do not always make for clean sheets. Yours is a *nostalgie de la boue*. Trouble will haunt your footsteps if you remain here, in the same way that revelation or largesse would a more fortunate man."

"Eh, your melon drama depresses me," my father quipped. "You're interested in how many cases of the fruit exactly? I don't know which is more galling: taking business advice from a pillock, or having travel plans thrown in with them."

2.
Somerleyton Rd. Brixton, London, England, 1965

THE AUGURIES OF MALBAR'S bibulous prophesying arrived in the summer of 1958 with the force of Edison's collapsing elephant, courtesy of an elaborately folded spheroid document tessellated with triangles and looking like a paper meteorite. I can only imagine – one is left little alternative with a pretender – my father's mental state when, clasped between his fingers of almost uniform length, flapped the monograph on which rested the source of his newfound apprehension.

The literature contained within the so-called *Sous-Futura* sent my father into a paranoid tailspin, doomed him to repeat past glories and maraud through a catalogue of memories in which he shared centre stage with famous Mauritian vandals. His adventures effectively ended, while the feats of derring-do folded in upon themselves like a Casela turtle guarding itself against mounting riders. He became obsessed instead with Sous protocol, engaging with it almost in an academic sense, detached and no longer applying its tenets to the thick of the shit of actual criminal enterprise. Even his charity work did not escape an early demise.

Most dramatically, it led to an exit from the island that he had called home for thirty-odd years. And while I recall very little from our tumultuous departure – a slew of boats, planes, way stations, and a ham-fisted pledge to a judge – I do recall that something had taken root in Serge's mind with a hitherto unknown fervency. No longer willing to engage himself in questionable behaviours, he instead began to recount the incidents of his youth, to me and to others alike, hoping to augment his stature in the eyes of the vaguely interested: how he, for example, once provided the voice of Doctor Koma on the banned wartime radio-serial "Narcoleptic Jenny" – whose shrill voice was heard echoing the lines at points of acute irritation, "Courts, sports, and genital warts! It's all gone to pieces!" – proved a noteworthy favourite among his new European neighbours in the early sixties, after he had made England our home for a few months.

Of course, a voice of contradiction scarcely existed for this well-heeled English audience – I couldn't say otherwise, remembering very little from my time in the country of my birth, cruel circumstance having cheated me of my birthright. Mauritius remained for them a locale of charming primitivism, Edenic by nature and uniquely out of reach. The array of well-wishers (most of whom were women that worked for the civil service, and who Sergent obsequiously courted in order to secure connections to gainful employment, improve my educational standing, and perhaps even provide me with a maternal influence), forced to endure the harsh scintillations of detail, found his pouring of a quart of milk down the small of his back to alleviate certain intolerable discomforts in poor and discreditable taste, however, and the dissonance of clinking glasses soon enlivened their disapproval. These missteps alienated my father's new associates, and he found himself more at home with Britain's own disenfranchised populace, its underclass helping the world turn from the shadows. An inspired storyteller is one thing, but the upper crust of society will not endure chicanery when they have nothing to gain from it.

One of those gaudy public showcases must have shaken me out of whatever childhood torpor I had been in and turned me on to the exact nature of my father's delicate psychic imbalance. His "condition" worsened, and it suddenly alarmed me that my father actually appeared incapable of commenting on new experiences because he became unwilling to put himself into new situations, beyond going to work anyway; his world was populated with episodes from the past, but no present could render the same service to the future. I wanted to know why he had uprooted us to go to a strange and unfamiliar country, why his mien took on the colour of the downcast penitent. Here in Brixton, he had no real possessions, preferring instead to live out of a Wheary wardrobe, a lifestyle which I had never been asked or consulted about how I felt on the matter, and being a far cry from the standard set in Port Louis. Why did we live this way? To go on his word on this matter was an exercise in vulgarity. Yet it was not uncommon for me to pursue an answer that seemed to lie with the unmentionable Futura:

"Where is the document? I wish to see it for myself."

"The document, as you call it," his common answer being, "has been destroyed."

"At least tell me what the final pages said."

"There are certain things a man hopes never to see, the decline of his triumphs chief among them."

Sensing his irritation, I would press on.

"Where did it come from?"

"From where does fate deal its deathblow? It does not matter – the damage is done."

"Malbar. He was trying to humiliate you. He was never a friend of yours."

"Old Faithful? He received the same document, but concerning him."

"Or someone is playing games with your lives," I suggested. "A common enemy. Or you both had the same idea at the same time for each other. Perhaps there was no document to begin with."

"You give us too much credit."

"Tell me the truth about what has gone on between you two. Why did you bring us here to this hateful country?

Think!"

After an agonizing period of introspection, which I would often mistake for the end of our discussion, my father would resume, on occasion many hours later, with small, almost unnoticeable explanations, such as,

"There is nothing to tell. I was a criminal one day, a citizen the next, just as he was once an officer."

"Evasion is your strong point."

"It should be yours. I could help."

I could have gone along with our peregrine unsettlements at first, but I needed a reason to go on. With my father's revelation of the existence of the Futura, I now needed to know if he knew about my mother's illness years before her symptoms first surfaced, and if the Futura could have allowed for time I could have made use of had he not squandered it. This was paramount and trumped any concern of where I fit in Serge's life, outside of a gangly-limbed inconvenience.

"Let me speak to Malbar."

"You are like an ant in an elephant's ear, pestering me unceasingly."

"The problem isn't that you are lying, but that you aren't saying anything at all. Subtle difference."

"You think I obscure the truth. But what I do is arrange reality in doses that are manageable. And I have learned to live with disappointment. You will learn to do the same."

"That is what you call manageable."

Eventually everything does come out, and the Futura, I would later be told, accounted for every criminally significant action he had taken since he was a child – even such actions that received no documentation by police. I recalled that in the first few days following his possession of the article in question, Serge had no personal interactions with Malbar or the Sous, refusing even assignments from the ganglords above him in the chain of command. He denied requests for alibis from other members, fearful of exciting the exactitude of the document's terrible scope. Later I heard that the Sous members spoke of it in hushed tones, positing that its danger lay not only in the mystery of its origins, but in the obstinacy of its purpose; in its ability to characterize the future to some implicit, exhortative end, before it was, as it were, inclined to happen. "Go straight," it seemed to beckon from beyond. "Go straight or face the teleology of the dirt nap!"

But nonsense has about itself the annoying ability of encouraging its own monolithic renewal: how typical then, that what began as little more than a rumour of predestination was now being handled with the care of the back-looking historian. There was even talk of this prognosticating document being distributed among the more resilient of the Sous Gang upon the completion of a "term in office." Cool heads here prevail against the assumption that there existed retired Souse around the world adhering to sacred itineraries and holy Baedekers, evolved from, some Sous could surely say, "divinely intervening effluences at work." Such a notion becomes too farfetched to entertain even for one's amusement.

It was only a matter of time before I ran into Malbar again, and I knew in advance the questions I'd put to him if he complied with my request for an audience. He had borne himself extremely well with me in the past, mild-mannered courtesy having in a way freed us from the bonds of unfamiliarity. So often had he been described to me as the knuckle-dragging sort of man – who preened when individuals condemned the drubbing their friends received by his hands, but ventured never so far as to come to blows with the steamrolling giant – that I must admit the prospect of a private meeting made my hands tremble. I was fortunate in never being confronted with this aspect of his personality in the past, and therefore enjoyed a liberality of language and insinuation. I would not go so far as to say that he took pleasure in our exchanges. I do not think it presumptuous, however, to think that he benefited from the exercise I afforded him: I mistook him neither for a child nor a fool.

I found him stepping out of a travel agency in Market Row, finalizing preparations to make his yearly return to Mauritius – a curious, unexplained habit that did not go unnoticed by the Sous who had witnessed firsthand his scornful remarks about his adopted country. He greeted me respectfully and invited me to dine with him at a nearby restaurant that we had both been fond of. I imagined that he would know all along that I had misgivings about bringing forward the subject which lately consumed my life, and that he would obviate windy formalities by breaking the ice. I imagined an interrogation along the familiar lines of

Question: Explain something to me, about the two of you.

Answer: What's troubling you?

Question: For starters, what business does a policeman have socializing with a base criminal? I don't understand the logic.

Answer: I hardly consider your father a criminal. For that matter, I hardly consider myself an officer of the law these days.

Question: He's told me some rather interesting things. You sent him the document?

Answer: You needn't take elaborate steps with me. You are referring to the Futura. Whether he has or has not divulged certain elements of our lives to you is not a consideration of mine when I am faced with your questions. I have nothing to hide. If you have a question, ask it directly, without guile.

Question: Will you tell me then if the Futura exists?

Answer: Yes.

Question: And?

Answer: It exists. It most certainly exists.

Question: Well, who was it that sent it?

Answer: Another man in uniform, undoubtedly.

Here Malbar would take a pinch of some rusty-coloured tobacco, or alternately pepper – depending on the particular turn of my imagination that day – to his nose and snort harder than I would think humanly possible. The conversation here would wax melancholic:

"Ti Pourri," I would recommend for indictment first.

"That would make the most sense."

"Oh, it's never the easiest way, never the answer we're most looking for with Sergent: Ti Pourri, the Derwish, the Bowling Green, all of whom I'd like to add live in the UK now. Given the subject under discussion, it's not very helpful or necessary to discuss matters possessed of sense, now is it?"

"It changed things between you, that cursed Futura. Can I ask you how exactly?"

"I think it would be more exact to say that we were placed on the axis of an upheaval that would have happened anyway. Over a barrel. The state of affairs we knew suddenly and impractically shifted. We had to adapt."

"It's as if you were never at opposite ends of the law. Like a right pair of Milk Duds."

"You realize that there cannot be one without the other. As soon as he was on his way, I was on mine."

"I don't believe that to be true. If there is no crime, I can appreciate that a policeman would be, as a matter of course, out of work. But the reverse can't be upheld. It doesn't work both ways. You're not saying everything."

"That's similar to something silly I once heard about the nature of truth and falsity, a subject with which you are more than superficially familiar. If there is no falsity, so the argument starts, then there can be no room, no reason, for truth; truth, as we are using it anyway, as that which corresponds to fact, buttresses itself against untruth. Truth as a derivative of the condition of not being false. You can imagine that your father could make a valid statement about his childhood only because he could alternately have made a false one. You follow? That is a simple point. To say that the opposite can exist, as you have just said, for the reason that there could be the condition of being false in the absence of truth – of being a criminal without my being an officer, if you prefer – is invalidly preposterous. A life of crime has meaning only in relation to the law. Put your reservations away. Even in telling the truth about telling a lie, or stealing so that you children will not grow hungry, there is in that both an element of truth and falsehood, law and chaos. To affirm that one can exist without the other is, with respect, a fool's comfort."

"I can only defer to your wisdom, naturally, but it's a mistake, I think, to associate truth, deceit, with policing and with illegality, as you have just done."

"Well then," he would say, growing very cross with me. "You can have it your way or you can have it mine; take my word that when your father stopped being a criminal, or when I stopped being a policeman, the other threw in the wet, dribbling towel. Or you can, if you feel it serves any purpose, leave it. What's your next bloody question?"

"It's as if you're proposing that if my father were to ever tell the truth . . ."

"Your father does tell the truth – granted in a very limited sense of the word. If I tell you the sun is blue, and you believe that what you behold before your very eyes is blue – and even if you don't – if I tell you and you affirm that you believe, when in point of fact you don't, then for the two of us, the sun is blue. You see? Because we can both experience the consequences of affirming that the sun is blue. We will be ridiculed like elephant ears together; we will be laughed at, drawn, quartered, carted away. There is truth, but not always happiness, in that – in consequence."

"That's a grim thing to believe in."

"You look at your father, and the extent to which you see truth is in the proposition, 'My father is a liar.' Li content sali nom dimoune; ça meme qui banne-la finne casse so la guelle. Does your father lie to get at truths or to get at fictions? That is at the heart of your questions.

(1:1.1) Your father lies on his Home Office skilled-worker application package.
(1:1.2) Your father is unqualified to work overseas.
(2:1.1) Your father receives his immigration papers.
(3:1.1) Therefore, your father is a qualified overseas worker.

"Tell me dear girl, which truth do you want? The world has not been sparing in that regard. I can give you economic truths, political truths, eternal truths even. But these will do you no good. Because in the end, there are no Truths, and there are no Falsities. There are no letters from forsaken enemies from a bygone era, no accounts of actionable behaviours. Only facts. Cold, falciform, drooping facts. And those disposed to use them."

Of course, the actual convention with Malbar proved far less illuminating, such was my dratted luck. I had correctly guessed that the Futura could be little else than a trumped-up reference to immigration papers – this much Malbar confirmed after a mouthy preamble that described the "conspiring forces casting their accounts with impunity, rolling loaded dice behind animated whistling, and engineering the perils of a thousand thundercracks lashing the earth's hide from the penumbral distance." He was not quite the muscle-bound brain my father had made him out to be, his reflections given life only when he sputtered about cutlets and strippers. Neither was he by any means unnaturally tall – childhood reminiscences having failed me once again – standing as a rather squat mushroom amid a gallery of weird, vegetative diners. No philosophical enquiry into the nature of truth, no mention of Sous pups or fruit gambits was forthcoming from his chapped lips. I devoted extra effort to understanding his Kreol, as he spoke barely a word of English (though his French was impeccable, strangely enough). The curdling arrangement of Kreol syllables swirled thickly like a bowl of porridge that had been left out too long, its surface belying a misshapen fragility. I asked which of my father's stories were true, which false, and he professed he knew nothing to that effect. There was little of the policeman left in him, no doubt dashed to smithereens, along with every other dream he'd harboured, by the asperities of disqualification. That my inquisitive nature was met with such industrious shoulder shrugging confirmed my belief that some element of his police training desperately remained intact within him.

His only remark to me before we parted was, "Li koze pou so la bouche pa senti pis" – roughly, "He speaks so his mouth don't stink." I never heard Malbar take a critical stance in my father's company, so I did not see why he'd start now in mine. A dig, no matter how true with regard to the subject of volubility, or however slight, was still at heart a dig. I knew what my father would say if the words had been spoken directly to him and the exact manner in which he would espouse them. That is more than what some get with their fathers, but the substance of a consolation should not rest in its ability to make one feel inadequate, I should think.

The meeting with Malbar had left me ample reason to take stock of what I knew: I had learned that there was nothing remotely extraordinary about the facets of the man I knew by a handful of different names, at least in the sense that he ate, slept, had, within reasonable limits of the word, "normal" relationships, and could be killed without recourse to silver bullets, the *Gáe Bulga*, or other miscellany salvaged from the world's scrap heap of ideas. My father did at one point take on for me greater proportions than existence willingly allowed him, stretching through his exertions the limits of life through dishonesty and a mastery of language. What struck me most, reading between Malbar's words, was that my father's decision to leave Mauritius wasn't entirely the result of a forced hand. Malbar described the immigration papers without the scantest trace of Serge's desperation, feelings which would naturally proceed from a hurried state of exigency.

I turned over the trivial question of what the greatest lie my father ever told was. I had heard some contend that convincing half the youth in Port Louis that virginities could only be lost on a single rumpled mattress in the Sous Gang's possession to be his crowning achievement. There are even those who would argue that Sergent's brilliance lay in persuading others that the Sous existed at all, that they were a vile surrogacy on which he could heap action after crime after lie, with something that could resemble ease. It's a trivial question because you cannot get a liar of this calibre to believe the truth, any more than you can one of his own lies. A liar usually gags on the truth, responds to its pungency with lurid outbursts. But Sergent thrived on truth too – or whatever popular consensus presented as truth – as well as on the ignorance of what it was. This was a man who would lie about knowing he was being lied to if it would somehow work to his advantage, who anticipated in turn people lying about lying about knowing they'd been lied to. His was a word that could not be trusted, or for that matter doubted, so strong was his devilish conviction.

Malbar never returned from his final trip to Mauritius. At the suggestion that he had gone off knowing that he had not long to live, my father said nothing, but instead reached into his pocket and handed me a gritty five-rupee coin, which felt heavy in my palms. I asked the ornery old goat if he wanted to be left alone and what he meant by the gesture, but met with silence, I handed the coin back. He held it between his thumb and little finger, twirling it restively, as though with significance. He smiled in a knowing way and chuckled as if he were the only person in the room, staring into the darkness, whispering, *"Montagnes pas zoine – dimounes zoine. Montagnes pas zoine – dimounes zoine."*

Mari la ek so madame p marche vers marchande volailles
so sarrette ki ena ene trone dorer couper en deux av milieu
avec deux trois fruits comme offrande. Marchande volailles
signale zotte are so la main pou dire zotte approcher· zotte
pose soupiere compote goyave avec precaution. Li faire
signe ki li accepter fruit la et li appelle ene serviteur pour
vine prend recipient ki encore tiede pou place li dan ene la
sam a coter lor n longue la table kot ena deza les zot
offrandes ki fine recevoir ce matin la. Serviteur retourner,
ferme la porte derriere li, pou empeche l'odeur ki sorti dan
l'usine la peau rentre dans la sam la. Marchande volailles
leve so paume la main ver le haut avec so bannes les doigts
en pointe. Li sacouille so la main pou ouvert so les doigts.
Couple la realiser ki zot fine gagne ene permission bien
rare pou zotte faire zotte demande.

Madame la commence dire, « nu ti content gagne ou
meilleur coq pou celebrer retour nu garçon. Li fine alle
vivre ene la vie en fou pas mal depi 5 ans. Sa bannes
goyaves la c'est ene cadeau de nu garçon et nu offert ou
sa comme cadeau ». Marchande volailles debouter et li alle
ver trone, so paletot salé ine maille lors ene coin chaise.
Tane ene boum et ene tipti hurlement de douleur. Li
retourner, checker si ena les dents mankés et donne
couple la 9 poulets sans plume attachés par zotte la
patte avec ene la corde. Madame la, bien content,
faire ene révérence en signe de respect et commence
sorti en dehors la sam la. Juste comma mari la pe
sorti dehors dan la bmiere ki pe pali li arreter et
li dire marchande volailles: « Ki garçon la ine faire
pou ki mou merite ene tel cadeau? Mo pas fine demande
9 poulets. Est-ce qui ou pe donne moi la viande gatée? »

Comma li dire sa, 2 gardes malicieux ki ti suivre marchande volailles dan la sam cot zot range tou bane offrandes, attrape sa couple la. Bane cadeaux la fine bien ranger zoli zoli lor la table la: halva, jaggery, cendol, barfi, colodent, rasgoula, Napolitaines, compote, tarte, claffloutis, broodpap, jalebi, yaourt, kulfimalai - tout avec ene variation de goyaves pour chaque plat. Marchande volailles prend ene cuiller de l'offrande ki couple la ine donne li et fonce fruit ~~~~ la dan so la bouche. Apres li crache li lor figure mari la et batte li avec ene gros di bois trouvé. << Moralité c'est pour bane montagne, étranger paley>> li dire mari la en baissant ver mari la ek so le corps cabosse cabosser. <<Dimoune pas assez fort danla la vie mais zot pas sa faible la ki zot pas capave montrer un peu respect dans la case lot dimoune.>>

Zotte fine charrier mari la dan ene couloir et jette li lors ene l'escalier. Li dégringoler et la li lagurre comma ene zanimo qui pas trouve clair pour regegne so l'équilibre avant ki li tombe lors ene trottoir pavé et dur, en roche plein ek taches, moville movillier. So madame ramasse bane zaffaires ki fine tombent de so poche et aide somari pou debouter. Zotte fine kitte sa tannerie la avec la chagrin dan les coeurs tandis ki derrière zotte ena ene tralee 9 poules morts p trainer dan la poussière et pe absorbe tou bane substance chimique ki pe deborde depi bane vats la chaux. La haut toit batiment, ti ena ene l'ombrage tout seul pe guette zotte, lerla li degazer descende lor plancher la chaux pou prend bane la viande ki pe colle lors ene liquide melange de l'huile ek savon. Li pena aucaine doute ki so retour pou celebrer exactement comma zotte finne promette li.

<u>Montagnes</u> pas zoine. <u>Dimounes</u> zoine.

3.
Sous fable, originally published 1944 in
Soustyricon newspaper

THE HUSBAND AND WIFE approached the gilt, spatch-cock throne of the pushcart poulterer with an offering of fruit. The poulterer waved them forward to her feet, where they placed the tureen of braised guavas. She signalled with a gesture that the fruit be accepted and removed to a banquet table in the adjoining room. A young attendant collected the warm container before placing it among all the other offerings that had been made that morning. The attendant returned, closing the door behind him, so that the odours of the tannery would not permeate the chamber. The poulterer held her palm upward with her fingers converging into a point, and then shook it so that the fingers expanded like a trap opening. The couple realized this to be a signal admission to hear their request.

The wife began by saying, "We desire your best capon to celebrate our son's return. He has been gone for nigh on five years into a life of reckless ruin. These guavas were a gift from him and we make them a gift to you." The poulterer stood up and weaved her way behind the throne chair, her mantelet snagging on one of its corners. A thump was heard from behind, followed by a howl of pain. She returned, checked her mouth for missing teeth, and extended nine featherless chickens to the couple, clasped together at the feet with a long piece of tether. Overjoyed, the wife bowed her head in respect, and began to walk out of the chamber room. Just as the husband was about to pass the threshold of the doorway into the fading light, he paused and addressed the poulterer as follows: "What's he done for you for us to deserve this indulgence? I didn't ask for nine chickens. Is this tainted meat you're offering me?"

Immediately, the couple were seized by two puckish guards who followed the poulterer into the room where all the offerings had been laid out. Decoratively arranged on the tables were every variety of halva, jaggery, cendol, barfi, colodent, rasgoula, napolitaine, compote, pie, clafloutis, broodpap, jalebi, yoghurt, kulfi – all with a guava-tinged variation to the respective dishes. The poulterer took a spoonful of the couple's offering and pressed the fruit deep within her mouth. She then hissed out its contents onto the husband's face and bowled him over with a dimpled blackjack. "Morality is for the mountains, fair stranger," she said bending over his crumpled frame. "People are made of thinner stuffs, but not so thin that we can't expect a little good courtesy in one's home."

The husband was carried forth along a corridor and thrown out across some steps, where he struggled like a purblind animal to regain his footing, before crashing onto a hard and wet theatre of stained paving stones. His wife collected the loose articles which had fallen out of his pockets and helped his broken body to his feet. They left the tannery ruefully, while behind them a trail of nine dead chickens collected dirt on the floor and absorbed the chemicals from overflowing liming vats. From the roof above them, a lone figure looked on, before descending hurriedly to the liming floor to grub up what meat he could that clung to the sticky fatliquoring oils, determined one way or another that his return would be celebrated in the exact manner he was promised.

Mountains don't meet. People meet.

4.

Blue Boar service station, Northamptonshire, England, 1965

WHEN THE CONDOLENCE NOTICES began arriving at our home, the effect of Malbar's death on my father became pronounced. His first feat of dissipation, outwith his immoderate drinking, was to buy a potato to which he applied a failing proficiency in woodworking to render a likeness of his departed comrade. The tribute lasted no longer than a few days before it began to fall in on itself and attract a battery of flies, then maggots, that were no doubt working the same deft magic some ten thousand kilometres away on the master copy. I was forbidden to remove this rotting effigy from the mantlepiece, and any attempt to reintegrate the mash-like features into the shape of a nose threatened outrage. On the day that I could no longer tolerate the putridity that now clung to the loose fibres of our clothing, and even befouled the reserves of the brazier, I carefully extracted and buried it by the retaining wall at the edge of the property line. I received such a thrashing that night that even Sergent could not help cradling my small, adolescent body as he removed the dirt and potato skins he'd earlier shovelled into my mouth. His rage was spent, shame now overtaking him.

The following morning I was rewarded, presumably in exchange for my silence, with sweets and a trip to the pictures. We watched the gaucherie of Norman Wisdom's *There Was a Crooked Man* (again . . .), which is as close to an apology as my father has ever brooked. Serge, unlike myself, was a nutter for all of Wisdom's films, especially anything that included Wisdom's one-man, pratfalling double act – his turn as Norman Pitkin and Giulio Napolitani in *On the Beat*, as Pitkin and General Schreiber in *The Square Peg*, as the entire cast of *Press for Time* . . . Which goes to show you to what extent I could cash in on this precious act of contrition.

Serge sat in the theatre taking notes, while I encountered twinges of recognition on the screen, regardless of which Wisdom picture we watched: wasn't Pourri wrongfully imprisoned by my father's hand like Davy Cooper in *Crooked Man*? Hadn't the Derwish once masqueraded as a priest to squeeze information out of someone à la *The Early Bird*? Didn't the Green look after a horse named Nellie? These connections never amounted to anything much in my mind; they were just stragglers of thought looking for a repository. The lights always came back on, and always we left the theatre with no further business. Like so many times before, we returned to the squat afterwards, only this time we had condolence notices to burn together. Then, we retired to our separate rooms.

When I awoke, my father was gone and did not return until after the sun had set on our little street. The sky out my window was littered with trembling celestials. Serge did not bother with his shoes and instead tracked in soot and mud and God knows what else over the living room moquette. He was soon bathed in the light of a dying flame. I had forgotten to extinguish the brazier and feared Sergent would come looking for me to exact a comeuppance a second time. The dimness in his eyes relieved me of my incertitude, for I could tell his mind was elsewhere. He held in his hands a sheet of paper torn into shreds. He threw the pieces into the fire. Without raising his head to look at me, he said, "We leave early in the morning. We won't be gone long." He then retreated back outside into the necropolitan darkness of the city, to prepare for the recondite business of tomorrow, locking the door behind him.

The following morning he roused me from my sleep with insistent shaking. He released my shoulder and placed a bag in front of me.

"It's packed with biscuits and fruit," he indicated. "Put anything else you want inside but leave me some room. We'll be home before nightfall. Five minutes."

After putting a few school books and some aniseed

twists in my bag, I dozed off on the floor by the base of my bed, then intermittently awoke on my father's shoulder as we descended the stairs leading out of our apartment. I finally found myself in the back of a car that looked somewhat familiar; it was filled with tarry faces, all of whom I recognized. To my right was the man whose moniker was the Bowling Green, a diminutive man with beak-like features who made his living in England as he did in Mauritius as a farrier. The Green was rechristened by my father because his given name, Sylvan, did not appositely convey his appreciation for an uncommon women's hair couture of the time. The Green's mother in this way had erred in naming him in tribute to his dead father whose life had been claimed too early on in the scheme of things. In front of me in the passenger's side was my father, who was fast asleep, and driving us to our destination while reading an eight-day-old newspaper was Ti Pourri, who unfortunately for all of us present, given his disinclination to bathe, had grown his hair out as an outward sign of acquiescence to the fashion of the time.

The beat-up Morris Minor slithered its way to a hasty stop at Watford Gap. Everyone got out except for me, but Sergent opened my door and bade me to follow him. In the time it took to unfasten my belt, Pourri and Green had gone inside, carrying a large canvas-covered object from the boot. Sergent took my hand and led me through the wide front entrance, where we weaved through a bevy of travellers, given that it was early in the day and a bank holiday. Inside the stuffy building, restaurants were arranged in such a way as to convey that no one gave a toss about anything; it rather seemed as if Charon himself had sneezed out the contents of his nose at the one corner of the earth where people cared even less about their surroundings than he did his own cheerless domain. Suddenly, in the back wall between two kiosks offering wrapped sandwiches and maps all along the M1, a door opened cautiously. A plump, mustachioed face poked through the crack and vengeful eyes flickered to life. Catching sight of the two of us, the head arched back like a viper, but before the door fastened shut, a polished winklepicker zipped out at the door's butt hinge.

Sergent picked at the handle, and making sure not to leave the door ajar, lifted me up over one of his arms and we sidled our way through together; he pulled the door back with vigour, snapping it shut. The craggiest set of misaligned teeth I ever beheld stared back at me. It made me think of war ration books and I asked myself why the owner still felt compelled to use them.

"Hello Derwish," Sergent greeted, extending his free hand.

"Have a seat, dingbat. I'll bring a stool for your little one," the Derwish replied coldly.

The stool was brought forward to one side of a large round table that had been worked over with knives, keys, and razor-edged fingernails. Green and Ti Pourri had already taken their seats, and once our refreshments (drinks of an unknown composition) were handed out, Derwish took his place beside his compotators.

"First District Sous Appellate Court now in session, the right honourable Black Derwish presiding," a voice from

43

beyond the vale of tears seemed to say, her head leaning back out of the range of the paraffin lamp that rested at the table's centre. "Also in attendance, Lord Justice Clerk Green, Clerk of the Privy Council Ti Pourri, and on loan from the secretariat's office, Sergent Mayacou. Also present, in unofficial capacity, two juveniles. Ahem."

I diverted my attention from these opening remarks and had it confirmed that the disembodied voice belonged to another girl who had been placed in a corner of the cramped storage room. In her hands rested a clacking Tomy Tutor Typer that accented the solemnity of the proceedings.

"On appeal on the order of Puisne Justice Madeaux," she continued. "Dated this June 17th. Pursuant to Malbar's final wishes, outlined in the last will and testament, we are gathered to take stock of its contents, debts, codicils, hereditament, hotchpot, and then finally, the division of assets. Lord Justice Clerk: the receipt of probate."

"Receipt of probate Derwish, your honourless," Green said.

"Thank you," the Derwish acknowledged.

The sloe-eyed girl in the corner of the room bore a strange likeness to the Derwish. She had the same jet-black hair, the same crooked posture; on the other hand, she had the Bowling Green's aquiline nose too, and the Green and Derwish being brothers-in-law, I assumed (correctly) a familial relationship. I waved at the girl across the table, who smiled diffidently at me in return. She hammered on over the stentorian voices of the assembled party.

"The floor is open to disputes to the articles contained

44

in the will and testament," the Derwish announced. "You have your mimeographed copies before you. You may begin. Madame speaker."

The Derwish's daughter (he gave himself away in the manner he phrased "Madame Speaker": familiar, imperious, disappointed) put away her Typer at his beckoning, and approached the table. She cleared her throat, remarking, "Petitionary motions now being accepted. Petitionary motions now being accepted."

The room acceded to her order. Sergent leaned forward on his elbows and addressed the girl.

"Thank you, Madame Speaker. Forgoing the event of intestacy, as I believe the document's veracity has been proven beyond a reasonable doubt, even if we haven't been able to locate Malbar's codex, I'd like to petition for the disbursement of Malbar's courtesies and goodwill. My understanding is that he has amassed a considerable fortune in favours."

"You shut the door after the steed is stolen, Sergent," Ti Pourri said weakly.

"No proverbs," Green droned. "First warning."

"I am in agreement with Pourri," Derwish said. "I won't countenance the motion – yet."

"Nonsense," my father went on. "The man is dead, last I checked. He'll be buried the way he wanted to be – to our financial misfortune, and in Green's case, his ruin – so I see no reason to help ceremony keep her frills on, when we all look to his assets covetously, one way or another. The Devil take the hindmost."

"Second warning," Green said.

My father nudged me; whoever broke the law last would suffer its injuries *in toto*, or so the game stipulated. The three other men looked about the room at each other, counting the seconds of respect for the departed. When ceremony was sufficiently given her due, they assented to my father's motion.

"The knocking shop," Green said.

"What about it?" my father asked.

"Eskiz mwa. I want Malbar's credit."

"That'll be the day. Amrita will tell you Malbar's credit is buried with him."

"I am owed two hundred quid, which he can no longer make good on."

"Derwish? Don't forget the priority of claims," Pourri said, remembering protocol after years of exile. He rejoiced at his own savviness almost superciliously.

Derwish leaned back in his seat and mentally consulted his knowledge of legal precedent.

"If Green thinks it in reciprocal equivalence, we cannot argue; he is the injured party, what? We can't have a whip round, now can we? All in favour of the motion passing?"

"Aye," hummed Green.

"Aye," Pourri repeated.

Thinking it a game, I raised my hand and mirrored the echo. The Derwish reached across the desk and slapped me across the face with enough force to hurl a volleyball across a car park.

"I'll not have my court made mockery of Sergent. Mo pa pou repeter."

Sergent pulled me close to his side and suffocated my

cries against his chest. He produced from his pocket a Barlow knife, extended the blade open, and placed the knife butt-first into my hand, putting pressure on my fingers over the thumb rise. I held it the way he wanted it manoeuvred.

"To tousse mo ti fi encore, mo pu casse to les reine, pilon," my father warned.

"Order, we want some order, please! No one will touch your daughter again, Sergent. We are among friends, or have we so soon forgotten?" Pourri said uselessly while the tension in the room stalked around corners. "Would one of Derwish's treasury stocks satisfy you? That sounds more than fair for the insult, eh Derwish?"

"If it will ensure violence is left at the door and if it acts in furtherance to the goals of the session, I see no reason why such a solution should not be encouraged," the Derwish said.

"Easy for you to say when you've got your licks in," my father concluded. "Move on then. Erezman toulmonde conne to fatigan."

"Trwazyem fois mon dire laisse ti enfants a lakaz," Derwish muttered. "Pe nas sulazman ici."

"I don't mean to prove countervailing Derwish, but it was you who put forward a regulation allowing children to be present at meetings on Cherelle's account."

The Derwish glowered at the Green.

"There is still the matter of naming his uh, spiritual successor," Green put forward hastily.

"Yes, I've given it some thought," Derwish began. "I think naturally the onus would fall on Sergent's shoulders.

47

You two were always closest in frame of mind."

A cloud of forced consternation spread over my father's features, settling like a shroud. He played his part and stymied the protest that raced to the edge of his lips. He simply looked at his peers to analyze the sway of opinion.

"You understand the responsibilities that would be conferred upon you, Serge, have not changed since Malbar bore them? Not to mention the benefits that would follow as well no doubt. It's fitting, however, since you made arrangements for Malbar to occupy the post for so long, that you carry on in his stead in the end."

My father did not answer the Derwish immediately, though his grinding teeth seemed to do that just as well.

"You know, we used to have a policy for decisions like this," Serge began. "Why aren't we drawing lots with caterpillar cocoons? Closest one to the butterfly loses . . ."

"Annual trips there and back so our supplies are well-stocked," the Derwish continued, taking no notice of my father. "On occasion you would be visiting South Africa and Réunion in lieu of Port Louis as well. Please be mindful of the restricted goods list before submitting a claim to the Office of the Exchequer. You will, in turn, be given notice if there is enough revenue for your quantity allocation. All in favour of Sergent's nomination?"

"Aye."

"Aye."

"Yea."

"Oh, bugger."

"You'll think twice now about ordering so many pounds of sausage, you stupid cadger," the Derwish said triumphantly.

The meeting was then adjourned for a thirty-minute recess while the men bought sandwiches or sorted the next cycle out at the launderette nearby. I was left alone with the Derwish's girl, who put away her things in a small, worn-looking knapsack. She was chomping away on a bag of nellikai berries as I slowly walked along the edge of the table and around to her side of the room, my fingers tracing the lines of the engraving burins.

"Pe nas trakase. I'm Cherelle," she said. I shoved her off her chair and she fell with a clattering thud. The shock of the fall overcame any instinct she might have had to cry.

"What the hell did you do that for? Gone soft?" she yelped.

"Who's your dad think he is to go slapping little girls around that don't belong to him?" I demanded.

I pulled out the Barlow knife and gummed up the Typer's keys through her sack. I hacked at the seams and slashed at the fine Shagreen hide. I kicked it about on the floor and heard the sound of gears and bolts flapping around like a grandfather clock being murdered. Then I retracted the blade back into the handle and put the knife away into my pocket.

"*Putain*," I scoffed. "That'll learn your stinking Derwish."

The men stooged around for a quarter of an hour before they returned to continue their proceedings, while I watched Cherelle simpering in a corner, holding the pieces of her typewriter in her hands. Occasionally she'd try lobbing one in my direction. Green entered the room like

49

a ramping ninny who'd realized he'd left the kettle boiling. He carefully set the kettle aside on the floor, and arranged the cups for tea without bothering with the washing-up first. He produced a single tea bag from a jetted pocket to make four cups with, before arranging the mugs in the order of the members' preferences. My father and the Derwish bickered briefly over the first and strongest cup, and then took their places once more around the pedestal table.

For the better part of three hours, the four claimants hemmed and hawed over various disputed articles and promissory notes, succeeding at times to determine a trickling train of preference. If my memory does not fail me, Sergent arranged notes written in blood on paper napkins, only to be obstructed by three more identical documents, all promising the same surety. Derwish in his turn tried to arbitrate matters concerning his own person, brokering satisfying resolutions in his favour. In Ti Pourri, all I saw was an exterior of calmness. If I had to guess, I would say Green merely wished to leave the proceedings without going home empty-handed.

I tried to remain as unobtrusive as I thought possible. Occasionally Cherelle and I were given perfunctory tasks that would help streamline the administration of the testator's wishes. We held up documents as the four men stared across at us earnestly. They would break their hunched huddle to place calls to different chapters and functionaries of the Sous gang, phoning home or to the north to gain a second opinion. In this way futures were bought and exchanged, souls were bartered like meagre scraps that were caught between the fangs of esurient beasts: Derwish took claim of the Sous stamp collection that belonged to Malbar, an assortment of self-pressed postage stamps that exclusively adorned gang-related correspondence and chronicled the exploits and history of the group visually. My father suspected the reason the Derwish made such a bold gambit was that the stamps contained commemorations of my father's successful candidacy for membership, as well as unflattering silhouettes of Malbar and Old Faithful to immortalize the former officer's own effective application.

The look on my father's face at this loss made me realize that he was there to lay claim to as many of Malbar's possessions as possible. He had great success in procuring Malbar's salacot, his stakes in the Sous jockey horse winnings, copies of classified police gang enforcement tactics that Malbar liberated from his former place of employ, a few of Malbar's molars that were knocked out when he was forced to surrender to beatings at the hands of Sous leaders to convince them of his devotion, and lastly, a worn-out Manurhin revolver. These items I was tasked with making room for in my bag.

The final item on the docket was the object rolled in painting canvas and tied together at both ends with baling wire that Green and Pourri had brought in. The four men leaned in at the table with their heels digging into the floor like tent stakes when I retrieved it from behind some boxes of loo paper. I immediately recognized this to be the *joyau de la couronne* of the evening. Cherelle, taking notice of the screeching chairs being pushed back by the four curving bodies, put her magazine away and stepped atop her stool.

"Guts, guts to open," she announced. "One ochre muslin mantelet, fallen into slight disuse."

Green was the first to speak.

"How the holy hell did he blag his way into possession of that?"

"It's a sight. I'd know it anywhere!" Derwish exclaimed.

"I don't care who knows it – we all lay equal claim to it," Sergent said stiffly.

"A monkey's tit it's an equal claim, kok depaille!" Derwish retorted. "Who here can lay a claim bigger than I can? I spent the most time under the Baba Yaga's wing, more than any of you!"

"Plug your ears girls," the Bowling Green cautioned.

"We could alternate possession," Ti Pourri suggested. "If the Derwish will have us."

Through half-covered ears, we heard that the well-travelled article was the fountainhead for years of raging, internecine jockeying between those in contention for it, chiefly because its history united the length and breadth of the Sous chronicle, forged as it was around the shoulders of a madwoman and in the crucible of her sickly armpits. Any child who wished to line their stomachs with the nourishing meat of a feathered fowl had only to agree to an exploitative contract written in blood with the poulterer's representatives; hoisting a small tumbril to their backs for the purposes of vending chicken was the sole obstacle to a towering hunger both replete and satisfied. To Malbar, the woman bore another connection though, having given him birth and thereby being furthermore his mother on a foul, stupid technicality. The furtherance of my father's designs on an empire of headless chickens seemed outwardly curbed by this hereditary title (not to mention a genuinely flourishing friendship), and a small, doubtlessly provident event caused a case of "double vision" – and again later in triplicate – to occur, which proved disastrous to more than one concerned party involved.

The poulterer began to be unable to distinguish between Malbar and my father, and later Malbar, my father, and the Derwish, who while fate deigned not to put on equal footing in terms of age or intelligence, saw fit to sponsor with nearly identical builds and statures. In this way, the three boys were positioned in a fractious *mise en abyme*, united in the way in which the poulterer doted on her "sons" and prepared meals for them. She even did three times the amount of washing! She thought her child the most capricious person imaginable for this reason, but somehow concretized their varying preferences, attributes, and annoyances into a unified individual. Malbar was content to share his mother's attentions with my father, but could not stomach the thought of the Derwish's mitts on any of his personal effects, partaking in any aspect of the life he rightfully called his own. It was possibly this thought which raced feverishly across my father's sensorium, the disgrace of it hardening his features.

"What do you mean 'If the Derwish will have us,' you cretin," my father said venomously. "You've got your histories mixed up."

The door through which we had entered burst open, shaking the fixtures on the walls. An arm disinclined to reveal the rest of itself held the door open, and a voice pronounced, "Ten minutes. And lug your garbage back with you this time." Without much fanfare, the door closed again, causing the glasses on the table to rattle around on the tea tray they'd arrived on.

"We'll have to resolve this quickly, if not permanently," my father said. "And don't forget the vig this time, Green. I don't want that idiot taking it out of my hide because you can't remember how to count."

"Look, Serge. What could you possibly want with that mangy shawl anyway? Cut seven cozies out of it for your daughter's tea party?" the Derwish japed.

"You mean on Cherelle's behalf, Derwishy-wash."

"I'll lay you odds on the next Sous tortoise race for it."

"I don't need your odds. The shawl is mine according to this codicil."

"Look, *un bras de fer*. For all the marbles."

"Of course, you lost them somewhere when you were young and want them back. Malbar gave the shawl to me. It's a lucky thing I bothered to read this hogwash. Go on and tell him, Green."

Green kept silent, while his face betrayed a look of incredulity.

"What's the shawl worth to you?" my father then asked the Derwish excitedly.

It looked like the Derwish had failed to consider this before, though I could not be sure. If I were him, anyway, I would not want to answer with haste and let someone else determine the touchstone against which I would barter. Fearing the Derwish was beginning to lose interest, however, my father spoke out of turn, so as to entice his competitor on to new acmes of foolishness.

"Maybe you should ask yourself if you can afford to let it slip out of your grasp?"

"You've brought your daughter along. This should tell me something."

"So did you."

"We know why Cherelle is here," Ti Pourri said matter-of-factly.

"She's here because I have no one else to look after her, you git. Or haven't you been paying attention these past few months?" my father blared.

Derwish's temper subsided at this point. He calmly turned to Cherelle and nudged his moustache to the left and right.

"*Du calme*. Let the last few remarks be stricken from the record."

Cherelle complied with her father's request and tore out the piece of paper from her minutes.

"Serge," the Derwish began. "I apologize. No one meant anything untoward with regard to . . . the unpleasantness that has occurred to your wife. Let us continue in much more civilized terms."

"Derwish, why don't we leave the formalities to les guels kok? I will allow one fair offer of exchange for the shawl – all you need to know is that it's something that holds value to me to be enough to satisfy you. If you insult my sense of fairness, or try to obtain it illicitly, you can be sure you'll never be able to confer it to any descendant. You know your brocards better than I do."

The Derwish thought long and intensely, and settled his gaze on what I was doing. I stood by my father's side and he had his arm around me again, clasped against my forearm. The Derwish then looked at Cherelle's bag, which bore the incisions I had made just a few moments ago. He lingered on the sapless state of this gunnysack.

"A stay of five years, the constitutional maximum, on your moon cursing. You've cheated an early death yet again, but the Menteur will have his due. They say knavery may serve for a turn."

"I'm not an idiot, pinere. I accept. Fine this man twenty quid – I grew sick of sententious bastards before he had the notion to scratch his own balls. Warnings have been given enough this session."

"Derwish, Kaartikeya. You are fined twenty pounds on the grounds of Article 5, whereby any act of expostulating moralization, whether in the form of adage, proverb, epigram, or any other form not otherwise specified here, against a member of the alliance is *an act of expostulating moralization against them all, and consequently they agree that each of them will assist the Party or Parties so attacked by taking forthwith, individually and in concert with other Parties, such action as it deems necessary to restore and maintain an atmosphere of* suggestive criminality."

"The one time you sticks-in-the-mud decide to put your heads above the parapet and it's for a punctilio. You plok poners are a real piece of work. Fine me your twenty quid then, but damn me if I won't have it out of your hides in one way or another! Mo pou zigeler toi!"

The Derwish and my father forthwith shook on their agreement, and signed a contract testifying as much in the company of all witnesses present. Derwish was brimming with excitement. He had made shift to conquer the obstacles before him. Cherelle and I were asked to undersign the contract, though on what grounds – certainly not on any authority anyone acknowledged – was not made explicit. We saw ourselves as having risen to prominence among these familiar men who factored so obtrusively in our lives; silent recognition passed between Cherelle and I, a recognition that immediately forgave the violence I had visited on her, I thought. She received this silent apology with equanimity. I handed her a peace offering from the recesses of my bag.

"What is this? Pareto optimality? Give me that," Sergent hooted.

He hoisted the guava out of her hands and deposited it in his mouth with satisfaction. He fingered out the seed and dropped it in Cherelle's open hand, which had remained hanging in the air.

"You're bound to be sick of those after eating a lifetime's worth, eh Cherelle?" my father joked. Cherelle's face worked itself into a pout as she heard these words.

I handed a fresh guava to Cherelle when Sergent's back was turned, and though what my father had said was likely to be true, she had manners enough to accept my gift graciously. I replaced the chair I was seated on in the corner where it had originally stood and waited along the crooked wainscoting of the wall opposite the doorway.

Serge was at the door having a few words with the custodian whose domain we presently occupied. He then stepped out, followed by Ti Pourri and Green. The Derwish glided his way toward his daughter and helped her collect her things along with the appurtenances of State left on the table. The last thing to be packed away was the poulterer's shawl, which the Derwish scrutinized in the dimness that now suffused the room.

"What the hell is the reason for it?" the Dewish asked himself, shaking the shawl open and closed as if he were setting a picnic blanket. "They're just leather samples stitched together . . . There must be an answer. Something I've overlooked. Ah-ha! Look at this, Cherelle. Her bookkeeping! Poor cow did have her wits about her after all. Mystery solved. Sylvan 06-09-44, Darlo 08-11-44 . . . There's me, Derwish 16-03-43, Malbar 23-05-41 . . . Ah, Sergent 26-09-54. I've got you dead to rights, gogote. He's always going on about seniority this, seniority that, when he's a decade short to be playing with the big boys. Eh, what's this? Sergent 26-09-44, Sergent 26-09-42! How can he have three inauguration dates?"

"I can tell you why," I peeped. "Because you blinked."

"What are you waiting around here for?" the Derwish said. "Royal assent?"

"Sorry about your bag, Cherelle," I said with contrition in my voice. "It was the Derwish's face I wanted."

The Derwish screwed up his face at the insult – as if someone were squeezing a grapefruit into his eyes. He was unaccustomed to being addressed that way by anyone, never mind by a child. He looked at the state of Cherelle's typewriter and made the connection. He turned to face me, where his mouth blossomed into a sinister grin.

"There may be a use for you after all," he said cryptically.

I sailed across the floor with a spring-heel and caught up with the others just as they were passing through the entrance doors. I hopped into the car last, as Serge had already made room in the boot for Malbar's effects and found his place in the passenger seat. Ti Pourri was the first to speak as the engine turned over.

"Where to now, boss?"

"Kettering first, then Uppingham. Might have time for Leicester too, but I'll not push my luck after that pretty pass. I can handle the rest on my own."

"You promised me the pistol," Green said.

"Here, it's not with the other things. Nobody wanted it anyway."

"Thanks, Serge. You're a top bloke."

"Pourri, take the car. Malbar wanted Simone to have it, but I doubt she'd have much use for it, much less know about it."

"His tart is getting most of his clothes," Green said bitterly. "It's all Simone bloody well cared about. What's she need a car for too?"

"You sure, Serge?" Pourri asked.

"You've earned it," my father replied.

"Don't think twice old man," Green interjected. "This old girl has a few sleepless nights left in her, that you can be sure of. Listen to that engine purr!"

"Thanks for helping with my reapplication after they

cashiered me," Pourri said. "I knew the Sous couldn't hold a grudge for long. Relatively."

"The rest of his birds are spread across London. There's no rush for them. What I can't do myself, I'll ring you up for. The heart wants what it wants, but someone has to foot the bill, as per usual."

"The Derwish will think we hatched it together if he's not satisfied with the shawl, Serge," Green opined. "We didn't exactly hide the fact we'd arrived together, now did we?"

"That's fine," my father responded. "I have the stay in writing now. It just means he won't be approaching any of you together in the future about what he thinks happened tonight. It'll be one at a time. Easier that way. To get your stories straight, I mean."

We didn't get all the way to Leicester before heading back home as planned. Tilting at my knees on the back seat, I could just see above my window out onto the numerous scenes that unfolded at every stop we made. Was I looking at my future? There were lissom women who tearfully accepted the gifts Malbar had bequeathed them. Some women hugged my father expressively, others shut the door on his face after receiving the parting gifts, and still Serge did not break the stolid composure he'd strangely arrived at on this occasion. We even made a trip to see my mum at Stone House, where my father left a parcel at the foot of her bed, as she was unresponsive to all of our attempts to communicate with her. I did not ask my father why Malbar had left her some of his belongings like the other bints. Several hours later, the car turned in on our street and careened to a half-hearted halt over the curb. Serge stepped out and moved to the back of the car to collect the things for which he had a use and which he believed Malbar would want him to have. I stood at our gate fiddling with a button on my coat.

"Your dad's a good man," Green testified, leaning his head out the window.

"No, he isn't," I said. "He's *non compos mentis*."

"Just because he don't pay you compliments, don't mean he don't love you."

Serge let me into the squat and then went back to the car. The final items he retrieved were two dead chickens that at some point between leaving our home and returning had their feathers removed. He held them squarely by their limp necks with his arms outstretched forward, as if he was leading (or ending, depending how you looked at it) a bathetic procession of the dead; and sure enough he walked through the apartment like a dread spectre haunting the abode and then exited out the kitchen into the back garden, where to my surprise, a primitive catafalque had been set up. It was composed of pieces of scrap metal and improvised guy-ropes cut from old rags. The decomposing potato lay at the centre of the bier, looking disconsolate. After placing the two chickens at the base of the elaborate arrangement, he pulled out two Cavenders from his pocket, placed them in his mouth, and lit them. He pulled a few drags from them before placing one cigarette in each of the dead chickens' beaks. The cigarettes kept tipping and falling out, and becoming fed up, my father rammed them down their gullets so that the beaks began to blacken from the ash. Their immobility during this sacrifice did not leave the chickens without an aspect of monastic beatitude. This covenant with the dead lasted little more than five minutes before it began to go pear-shaped. Bugs started noticing the offerings, neighbours began wondering aloud where that awful smell of incense was coming from. I knelt on the grass to remove the chickens at the conclusion of the ceremony, as it did not seem appropriate for them to go to waste, or worse, attract the attention of the rabbits. Serge gently laid his hands on my neck and told to me stand up. He shook his head to indicate that I should leave them there, come what may. When we were back inside the house, he went to the mantlepiece and handed me a small package wrapped in newspaper and twine.

"It's from Malbar," he said. "I didn't know he cared, but there you go."

I tore at the package quickly, leaving the wrapping at my feet. Between my fingers was a miniscule, hand-bound book whose dimensions couldn't be more than a few inches square. I leafed through its pages quickly, and inscribed within it in an almost illegible, Liliputian-like scrawl, I made out the headings of practices, codes of conduct, and recorded exploits of the Sous gang since its lowly inception as a band of outrageous chicken touts. Inspecting the cover more closely, I realized that emblazoned on it were the words "Souslard avant sous terre." Before I could engross myself further, I had the sense of being scrutinized by Serge, and so I shut the codex.

An overdue sense of boredom set in, and though the feeling had lain dormant within me, it took holding the object of such searching to realize that I did not care about it anymore; and that quite possibly, the years of my father's coyness served to stamp out all my curiosity and supplant it with articulate dejection. That Malbar was the one who took notice of my unhappiness, and not my father, only furthered my indifference to the Sous.

I placed the codex in my back pocket and stomped up the stairs, thinking to myself that I no longer was bothered about what kind of person my father was, or who he associated with, or to what ends he still attended his ridiculous meetings on other continents, whose distance alone seemingly rendered their actions and discussions the tincture of folly. All that preoccupied me at that moment was how Sergent was nothing like Giulio Napolitani any more than Malbar was like Wisdom's alter ego Norman Pitkin – the Liar and the Bobby were just stories, stories that held nothing over the present, regardless of their entrenched basis in the past, reflexively infused by cinematic power so that these two men could forget that they were now just a pack of dodos in a country that would like to scrub them off the soles of its dignified feet. The Sous were never fingered for a crime here, never martyred for the sake of the greater good, and more importantly, never late for the Yard because they pinched an innocent man on the Tube; never thought to use a hair salon as a front for an Italian jewel gang – either a neither. *Either* of them being *neither* the other, because they were lost in the paradox of their brittle rivalry. I learned to say goodbye to one history and grew to bridle against the draggled strands of another, or so some could say.

5.

Flaxman Rd. Brixton, London, England, 1970

AFTER SEVENTEEN MONTHS in Exeter, then four in Staffordshire, there followed half a year in a parky bedsit in South Harrow, ending finally in a doomed stint back in Loughborough Junction. I was on my back foot and packed with my gear, was to stay with the only family I knew to bear a loose relation to on the other side of the world. Everything was arranged very hush-like, while Serge took an early bath from the Chalk Farm turntable he was working at renovating. Expected back in Port Louis, Serge said things would get squared between us despite the travel visa papers humming an elegiac salute to expulsion. We moved fast in the few days left us, selling off our things as best we could, which meant for practically any amount below asking. Serge had been prepping the floors of the turntable for striated-tile conversion, or some such thing. Someone had the bright idea to forgo the mineral spirits entirely and accelerated the job by using flame-throwers to heat up the tar beneath the old flooring. I could tell Serge had a hand in this because he and his mate would collect the tar by the chuckful and sell it off to longshoremen who might want to use it for oakum or peddle it as cheap, unreliable sealant for boats. I couldn't be bothered to find out. Off his nut Serge was, completely – but wellspring of a good motive it was hard to say otherwise.

As I said, it was my last day before I was supposed to fly out to stay with one of Serge's bimbos he busied himself with while my mother was in Stone House getting sterilized and rubbed up by other patients. Serge said there wouldn't be time or money to see her off this time; that she wouldn't notice to begin with. There was always time, he said, time most of all to make up for time lost later on. That was always in our abundance.

I had a handful of *Knockouts* in my bag, my plane ticket, passport, and Malbar's codex. I checked my things every now and then to make sure they were still there. There was always the niggling feeling before a trip that it had all withered away somehow and was only kept intact by repeated rootings and analysis. I was with my mates Christian and Annaleigh, who were brother and sister, in Brockwell Park while their otterhound Scooter was not half-mucking about as much as we usually gave him credit for, chasing the passersby. I promised Chris and Anna I would write them. They knew how much I hated sitting still for anything though and so we were making the very best of whatever teeny-weeny gobs of time we had left. I gave Christian all of my 45s and Annaleigh my air-guns I'd collected in the past year. It would be an impossible collection to rebuild in Canada. Generally a very sad time for us, all in all; it was patched with silences of every knowable variety, but we were enjoying the sandwiches their mum had packed for us to no end all the same.

It always made me sad that I could never seem to hold on to anyone for longer than a fixed span of time, a few months tops, except old Serge. Even when I told myself that not all relationships were meant to stand shoulder to shoulder into the Eternal and that the longing I felt was normal, I still felt an incompleteness in my heart on account of the fact that I wouldn't continue to see Chris and Anna. I was in this mercurial frame of mind when we saw the horrendous accident. A motorcyclist got ramrodded by a weaving motor that failed to come to a full stop. The cyclist made a churning arc in the sky like a plastic soldier you'd just flicked with your thumb, while the Bug started to brake; soon thinking better of it, the driver then hammered the gas and turned down a narrow ginnel screeching metal and sparks all the way in like a tight bugger. The sound of backfiring thunder was already turning into an echo before the body slammed onto the paved road. It was like the sound of a hundred doorknobs clattering in a rucksack as they skidded down a flight of stairs.

Christian was first on his feet. Scooter followed shortly

afterwards, while Annaleigh and I tarried a bit to collect the most important valuables about us, she her shoes and myself my pack and my glasses. You developed this kind of hesitancy when you grew up the way we did, always a look over the shoulder, even when you witness someone a touch from joining the great majority. When we reached him, Christian was kneeling over the body trying to un-fasten the woman's helmet from her head. The way it had been impacted into her face, I could tell what was left of her jaw was obstructing her breathing, which came out a suppressed whistle.

"It's stuck. I think she's going to choke," Christian said.

"I'll get some help." Annaleigh let her feet carry her away, leaving Christian and I to wonder over things.

"The bastard . . ." Christian muttered. "Don't worry, help's coming."

Even as he said this, I could see the skittering regret in her eyes. She could tell by the look on my face that our sooty mugs would be the last, unfamiliar sight she'd have to take away with her. Some comfort. This was running through my head as we saw the life slowly ebb away from her body.

"She's gone, Chris," I said respectfully.

"Yeah."

"Let's have a look."

I reached inside her jacket looking for a pocket and Christian slapped my hand away. He didn't say anything, but his eyes remained fixed on me. It was as if he was see-ing me for the first time; as if I was coming undone. Some people finally hobbled close enough to see us through the dusk. Their spindly legs marching through the park looked like a stop-motion dinosaur.

"What's happened?" came a sharp, insolent voice belonging to a bearded man. His wife was tugging away at his arm, trying to keep up with his adiposed strides.

"That bloomin' wog was thieving her pockets," a crone replied from out of nowhere. "I just seen it."

"You've gone dotty," I said, arching my back with honesty.

Christian regarded me something unfriendly. I reached again in the pocket and this time he tipped me flat on my back, righteousness informing his movements.

"Gor, Chris! Not you as well."

"You better get out of here before you spoil it for yourself," Chris advised.

"Now, now lass, don't listen to your friend," the beard's wife cautioned in her tipsy bedside manner. "You'd best stay right where you are until the old bill arrive. They'll have some questions for you both."

"Chris, the woman's got identification!" I implored.

Annaleigh came back out of breath and leaned down beside us.

"Meat wagon's on its way," she said, before catching on to the situation developing. "What's going on?"

"Miss, do you know these two?" said the beard. "You'd best start from the beginning."

"There was an accident with a motor," I began.

"No," the crone interrupted. "Not you. The other girl."

"What did you do, R –" Anna started asking.

"Shut it, Anna," Christian ordered. "Get out of here

if you know what's good for you. I won't tell you again. Don't throw it away."

Scooter began to whine plaintively. I realized I'd fallen on him when Christian pushed me. I pulled my weight edgewise off him and held him close by my side. Scooter looked around quizzically, uncertain of the atmosphere building, bless his stupid animal heart.

"Grab her," the beard said, directing some louts who were coming our way like rotating skittle pins, they were so pissed.

I took one last look at my friends and thought about the lasting impression I would leave on them; how that would last forever and how the explanations I might write in the future would be for nought. Chris had made up his mind already and Anna, though the more sympathetic of the two, would come around eventually, especially given how much she craved her brother's approval. I picked myself up and fastened the straps of my bag. Then I dashed in the opposite direction for home.

When I got in, Serge was mashing the tea. He could see the tears streaming from my eyes. He said nothing. It was evident that he wasn't surprised by anything, as if he knew the final outing with my mates could end in nothing but misery. For all I knew, he'd just gone through the same thing. He set the cups on the table. I collapsed on the couch and picked at the scabs on my knuckles.

"*Couillon*, it's getting cold," my father instructed, beckoning me to the arranged table.

I sat still for a moment, envisioning an alternate day's end. Then I crossed the living room to the table, where I sat across from him.

"Eat your scoff. To faim?" he asked.

"No."

"Cot to billet?"

"I have it. Terminal 3."

"I'll see you as soon as I can. The tar money is running out, but once I get to Beau Bassin . . . I'll pull some strings and fly out to meet you. Six months."

"Okay. Six months."

"Listen to me. You can't stay with Marjorie for long. I promised her no more than a few weeks. You're going to have to find work as quick as you can. Dogsbody, grounds-keeping, what have you. You're old enough now. Forget your A-Levels. Until I can come get you anyway."

"Right."

"Bit of advice. Don't stick out. They'll stick you right back in."

"I will do."

"And don't mend fences with cretins. They are counting on like-for-like sales. Good night. Safe travels."

I rose and left my half-empty cup on the table. I took out a pen and some scraps of paper from a drawer. I started writing a letter pressed against the top of my thigh, addressed to Christian and Annaleigh. The words had a great unwillingness coming out, as if they would never forgive me for giving them voice. I thought again about clearing my name, then about lying and putting things in a perspective they might actually be disposed to understand. But I abandoned the idea altogether and thought better of it; thought better of ever being understood, or of ever being given a fair shake. The lost art of giving people exactly what they wanted was an overfilling cup of dudgeon. I did not want this for myself, but I would give it to them anyway. And I would make it in any way I could my own. I would become those parallel thoughts which reposed in Christian's mind and in the housings of the mob, resolving the history of my poor, barmy mum's sickness, my last night in England, and the rough idea that I had nothing left to lose, into the idea they had of me. Roll up every secret confidence and history of my life I ever vouchsafed which Christian turned to form the picture of my kind – a penniless wog who thought I was owed something for everything I ever did. For what was stolen from me, for what was never given to me this night, I would make everyone the worse for it.

6.

Phenomenology of the Mind's Eye, North End, Hamilton, Canada, 1974

IN THE ALTERNATE UNIVERSE where I continue my schooling in England and my father doesn't abandon me in a godforsaken country I know nothing about, I am slightly less irritated than the situation I presently find myself in. My mother is miraculously cured of her ailments and is discharged from heaven-giving Stone House. We are reunited as a family and Serge no longer needs to continue a life of reckless ruin. Somehow he manages to extricate himself from the Sous without retaliation of loss of limb. They buy a nice house in the country, or what passes for it these days, somewhere grand like Knebworth or Ballasalla. Things could be worse. Serge becomes a local celebrity with timeworn tales of inaction and subterfuge, eventually netting cool millions selling his story to the television networks. "My father used to run around in the mid-Twenties with a group of hustling powderpuffs called the Wigwams, a name whose derivation was the subject of cankerous, uninhibited ridicule." My mother for a time stays home where we can properly become acquainted. She takes an active interest in what I am studying; I like French and English literature the best, followed by natural sciences, philosophy, maths, and geography, in that order. When our relationship is such that we can tolerate long absences from one another, even after practically half a lifetime of it, she takes on a job at a public relations firm handling cases of the highest order. She is allowed a professional life and I am granted teenage heartache, pissy tantrums of the warbliest order – colours not being bright enough, wrong brand of foodstuffs, non-quality makes, and the like. I am miserable this time 'round because the hot toddy is not warm enough, glory be. But our company improves, as it soon includes Stewart Granger, Jerry Desmonde, and other gascons of British renown, on account of both my parents' social calendar. Jerry calls me "Roundelay" as a pet name. Everything is in frightful good order.

We all begin to speak with finer accents too, the mark of real class. Serge drives a Silver Cloud and he's not chauffeuring anyone around neither. He also has a Silver Shadow in his possession, parked in a clearing in the middle of the bosky wilderness that abuts against the property, although he does not like that as much and prefers to keep it hidden. The milieu we now find ourselves in helps us tune in at the right frequency. I never have to hear the Derwish's soppy-toned voice or the Green's butchering of Latinate syllables. They keep out of our lives and we theirs. All is right with the world, and it keeps on turning.

There is one rule in Serge and Virma's household and one rule alone, and that is to never go near the codex, which is housed in a fire-resistant vault, entry to which is accessed via a spiral staircase, a gift of design made to us by Alan Fletcher. The codex in the wrong hands will send vibrations along a fault line of the past; it will rewrite our perfect future, and send us back to that broken universe of indigence and scandal-mongering. So beware, fellow-travellers of the self. The codex has that power, that re-barbative aptitude for realization. It can predict your destinies as much as it can ensnare unsuspecting readers to its torments. This is why it is kept in our possession for safekeeping. The Sous want their oracle back. They want to claim for themselves what is rightfully ours. But we can see them coming. And we should continue to see them coming from any and all directions, every and all times.

I never consult the codex in this suture of a future coming quarrelsomely undone though – the codex which was to preserve the harmony of an eldritch perfection. So much for happiness then. Maybe the codex has come up against other competing codices that outline the Derwish or Green's overlapping narratives against ours; I don't know if it will cling on to the meaning formerly betrothed to it, or settle for becoming a wish-book of pipe dreams and a dramaturgy of unfulfilled potential held close to the breast where it can work its insuperably benign magic. I never was a dab hand at thinking ahead.

The latter I can live with because I am known to respect privacy with a withdrawing secrecy. No good reason to violate the sacred charge with which Malbar entrusted me or wished to answer the questions I first posed him about Serge. If the book is a fabrication, worked out by Sergent's hand to tide me over, the conscious self of supressed memory, limited possibility, and the strictures of the real world does not show immediate signs of acknowledging the idea. It serves a better purpose, as a best-case scenario, to regard the codex as the only act of unadulterated compassion ever made to my person without an expectation of return, and as a queer sort of talisman as a worst case. Bully for me and for history then! Time still shunts forward like Crisco sliding down the caruncles of a Grand Menaceur . . .

7.

The Kadadac Bar, North End, Hamilton, Canada, 1974

I KICKED THE STONE along the pavement for as long as I could, moving at a cross-purposes to the way leading over to Marjorie's. After having been pelted in the head with it by fleeing vagrants, I was in no mood to receive her tinny, ninny-braying again. Damn the ogre-woman and her crumbling dosshouse for the strange and neglected. I was out of sorts before I even found myself at her front step, littered with its windswept rubbish and gnarled weeds growing through cracks in the pavestones, because I could not remember what I had been thinking about prior to the welt growing at the base of my skull. I looked over my shoulder before going through the front door.

There was a muddy splendour of shoes; no doubt we had unexpected company. I heard the bottom-weighted sound of a bottle snapping sharply over the countertop, the scuttling of footsteps following after it. Marjorie poised herself between the entranceway separating the drawing room from the cloakroom. I could make out the fuzzing indistinctness of a shadow by the inglenook, but could not place exactly who was standing there.

"We expected you at noon," said Marjorie.

"Expect on expecting on then. Who said I was staying?"

Marjorie clicked her tongue unimpressedly before swivelling around and looking into the direction of the person hidden from view. Her face seemed to say, "You have a go then." I walked through the doorway and saw the Bowling Green fidgeting with a herringbone cap in his hands. He was both shoeless and sockless, airing the travels out of his toes. That man: his tousled hair looked like an elephant's graveyard in monsoon season, which was half-combed for half of appearance's sake.

"Hullo, cookie," he cooed softly. "Give us a kiss?"

I assented. I gave him a peck on both his cheeks. He received me in an unlecherous fashion, if such a thing existed in mankind. He was totally unversed in the matters of the flesh. He always looked as if he was waiting for you to call him to the head of class for recitation.

"Why don't you get ready for work?" Green said. "There'll be a surprise waiting for you."

Not even two weeks had passed at Marjorie's before I was raring to go – to get out I mean. Now, it had been years since Serge had told me to pack it in as his daughter and to have a go at my lonesome, so I thought to myself that he had squared everything that was worth squaring between the Derwish and him, and maybe my father could reenter my life if his nomadic travels came to an end – bit strange in any event, that for someone who excelled in his affairs, he could fail so extraordinarily in evading a sentence of endless smuggling that proved so disagreeable for all concerned (even considering the rough-patched funk of enervation he fell into in the Sixties, letting someone hold so much over his head was bizarre and out of step). Finally, I thought, I could leave Marjorie's smelly, crammed-in manse.

I raced out of Green's arms and into the kitchen, expecting to see Serge's gorilla hands at the icebox. I ignored the sign on the door and pushed past the entrance forcefully; it wheezed on its hinges like a smoker's cough plugged up with bile. The door knocked a few pots off their hooks on its way back to the starting point.

"What are *you* doing here?" I asked, trying to mask my biblically proportioned disappointment.

Cherelle sat on a short stool filing her nails. She put out a hand for me.

"What can I say? I'm a glutton for mistreatment. No tricks this time?"

I took her hand stiffly to make a sign that I would make a decent go of it this time.

"We'll get on as far as getting on's possible."

"Scout's honour?"

"Something like that. Well then, how have you been?"

"Same difference. Here, take one?"

She handed me a long-stemmed, spongey, deracinated stick of sick.

"What the hell are you eating?"

"It's a dried placenta. It'll even you out, believe me. Go on, have one."

"Where did y . . . Never mind. You're disgusting. That's foul in four different area codes. Who would have it off with you?"

"Don't you want to have kids someday? This will have caramel coming out your tits, not to mention improve your chances. It can't hurt you none."

I would have taken this the wrong way, but I sensed in Cherelle an overweening desire to please. I felt like I owed it to appease her. It couldn't have been any easier being the Derwish's monkey than Serge's.

"Coming close only counts for hand grenades then," I said, munching on the chewy assortment of bits. "I'll have you answer for my chances then if I come up short in about forty years."

"Don't be so sure about that. I'll leave the bag with you and you can take more whenever you get hungry."

Marjorie poked her head in the kitchen.

"No roughhouse, girls!" Marjorie rasped, responding to the noise earlier. "You've got regulars. Are you here or aren't you?"

"I'm here, I'm here!" I grumbled. "What's she doing here?"

"Because you can't mix a drink worth a damn."

"Yadda yadda yadda. Keep your knickers on. Oh I forget, tarts don't wear any!"

A few moments later, Cherelle and I shuffled out of the kitchen each carrying a tray of cutlery for behind the quartz-covered bar. Green was sitting on one of the stools, chewing on a toothpick and talking something over with Marjorie, who had locked eyes with him. There were a few other patrons at tables, but none that I recognized. The bar was closed off except for Green and another man. When we were halfway ready to go, Cherelle addressed the Green; she was a natural, like she'd been mixing drinks for the Derwish and uncle Greenie since the dawn of exploitation.

"I'll have a grasshopper to start, then a shandygaff with Stoney if you have it."

We obeyed, as was our custom, to the letter when possible. Green knocked back both drinks with gusto.

"Have another?" Cherelle asked timorously.

"I'm alright, dear. We're here on business, so it's Act of the Apostles for us."

I didn't know what he meant, but at a quarter after the hour, the front door opened rather brusquely, and in walked the morosest-looking fellow you ever laid your sorry eyes on, assisted in his movements by two four-pronged walking sticks in each hand. He was youngish, but his features had a worn-out, if dignified quality. There was no truckle bed for the head on those shoulders. He spun little half-moon crescents with his sticks each time he put a hand and foot forward, his rugby ball of a head looking like it was being pinched by both sides between invisible thighs. He also carried in his teeth the handle of a large and unwieldy portfolio case. He hobbled around the foyer for a spell, intent on settling at the bar, but still made a show of taking slow stock of the windows and paintings on the wall. There were portraits of Guillaume Dufresne d'Arsel, Ramgoolam, Paul Bérenger, and other Mauritian politicians scattered around the Kadadac. "What is this, the National Portrait Gallery?" his furrowed brow was sort of implying. The Roundman spat at the sight of Bérenger, miraculously through the handle hanging out from his jaw, before making his way to the bar in his tumble-dry fashion.

"Pour commencer, j'aimerai avoir six napolitaines, trois co-telettes de poulet," the Roundman started, addressing everyone behind the bar. *"Et vous pouvez laisser la bouteille de vinaigre et du sirop d'érable."*

"To pu mange tout sa la?" Cherelle asked.

"Hmmph. Zot pas apprane Francais ici dans Canada?"

"She don't speak French so good as you, shit-for-bones," Green said. "She's just trying to be friendly. No reason to get shirty. Play nicely, then."

The Roundman rotated his stool to face Green. The incommoded body threatened confrontation: his spine was propped as high as it would go and his knuckles faced out on the bar and over one of his sticks. He was the cruciform version of put-up-your-dukes, what good it would do him. At the sight of the Green, he flushed in his face and relaxed his body into a torpid mass of flesh that sunk down into his sides and shoes.

"B-bowling Green," he gibbered to himself.

"Michel, right? We spoke on the phone. What line of

work did you say you were in again? Speak English by the way, if you don't want them to understand you," Green warned, his eyes passing over Cherelle, Marjorie, and myself, but resting on me especially with implicit design in his expression.

The Roundman was having trouble catching his breath, and between gasps of air, he fitfully managed outbursts of adulation and worship. The Green took it in stride – where else would he get that kind of attention? – sneering with his toothpick, which was looking more and more like a conductor's baton orchestrating a menhir arrangement from the unenthused space between his front teeth. I was cutting my fingernails with Cherelle's clipper, my head bent down low, but I nevertheless kept watch of the two men. The ears and the corners of my eyes had some of the best seats in the house.

"I'm a solicitor. A-acquisitions and conveyancing primarily. The matter at hand?"

"Wait a minute. You don't mind, do you?"

Cherelle came around the bar and patted the man down, inspecting the walking sticks. When given the all clear, the Roundman produced his brown portfolio for all to see. He opened the cover and began to turn its pages delicately with a pair of tweezers, which revealed a trove of Mauritian souvenirs produced by the Sous, the likes of which were likely never to have been seen outside of official Sous functions. There were clippings, drawings, advertisements, posters to Sous events, Sous stamps torn off of envelopes, schematics for light and sound machines, and other rarefied memorabilia. The case was a gushing rainbow of memories from the gutter, glittering on their way to the raised relief of our minds.

"Interesting," began the Green. "You even have copies of the *Soustyricon*, our local newspaper. We are very particular about who has access to this, Michel. You can't exactly run to the corner to get them."

"Y-yes, procuring those items," the Roundman stammered. "Very tricky."

"Darlo? Come here a moment. You won't mind if my associate verifies the probenance of these papers? You never can be too sure."

The man had gone virtually unnoticed at the opposite end of the bar until the Green beckoned him. He had the kind of face you wanted to forget soon after seeing it, it seemed to signify so comprehensively absolutely nothing at all. Like a head composed of wet sand (or a mutilated potato might be more for it), it was blank and expressionless. He pushed his glass away and approached the two men with a stalking kind of gait. Though middle-aged, he was something of a peak specimen as far as primed human action was concerned – a force to be reckoned with if only given the occasion.

"So where did you say you got them?" Darlo thrummed.

"Most of it there, some of it here."

The Green and Darlo darted hurt looks at Marjorie.

"Not here, in the Kadadac. I meant Canada, generally."

"Of course, of course," said the Green, sounding a bit reassured and toneless at the same time.

"There's a lot of the Menteur's things here," observed Darlo, though when he had an opportunity to survey the case's contents was anybody's guess, as he had not moved his trained eyes from the Roundman's face. His hands crinkled a few papers and artifacts blindly.

"He is undoubtedly the most interesting of your group, no offense to present company. Violence and the threat of violence, it doesn't require a lot of subtlety – it's a mug's game. What the Menteur does, it's . . . it's like the breath of a hurricane. It's a force of nature."

The Green let out a chuckle as I handed out some food. I scrawled on a napkin the words,

AND HE CAN BLOW LIFE INTO DEAD CHICKENS TOO

so that only the Green could see. He took out a pen and made some notes in a leather-bound book that he had with him.

I was so fully engaged with the conversation before me that I just barely noticed the little shots of electricity I started feeling being pulled out from my extremities. I recall now the feeling of having swallowed a pencil in the right side of my throat, as if someone were sitting on my back. Cherelle was the same with regard to her engaged attention, minus the bit about her body turning in on itself, which I couldn't be sure of one way or another. I never actually did see her *consume* any of those beastly looking things. In any case, the placenta was clearly not agreeing with me, giving me brief spells of nausea. I entertained the thought that Cherelle had poisoned me, or that it was some kind of blamed food allergy, but soon ignored it, pushing through the new sensations. I was desperate for any news of my father's whereabouts and had good reason to suspect he would come up as a topic of conversation sooner or later.

"He'd like that, Michel, he really would. Okay, nitty gritty: what are you asking for the lot?"

"Oh I think you misunderstand me, Green. I'm –"

"*Please*. Sylvan. The name is Sylvan."

"Sylvan. A pleasure. As I was saying, you misunderstand me. I'm not here to sell any of these items. I could hardly bring myself to take them along with me here today if not for the uh, auspiciousness of the gathering."

"I don't understand. If you're not here to sell them, then what are we meeting for?"

"I wanted to learn about the items in detail, fill in some of the lacunae. Where this photo of you and Pourri was taken, for example. And whether this is an authenticated square of the Sous mattress, if my transcriptions of the Sous anthem are correct, going by ear. So many questions that need answering. It would be an honour."

"Let us see what you have for us here then."

Darlo was now pantomiming behind the Roundman, trying to figure out if he would be up to the task of dragging the body to the backroom. His hands were full-nelsoning the space a few feet behind the Roundman, the breadth of his arms getting wider and wider each time he took a step forward. In the course of these measurements, whenever Darlo tilted his head back and closed one eye like an urban planner for the devil's geography, he looked more the fool. All he was missing was a T-square slung out of his pocket.

"Look at his fizzog, he's right pleased with himself!" Darlo mused aloud, resuming his original position at the bar before the Roundman could catch on.

"You've almost got this bit right, Michel," Green said, looking at the relevant document from the Roundman's dragon horde of memorabilia. "The anthem goes 'Aka aka *boule* caca, not 'Aka aka *roule* caca.' The difference mattered to Serge, anyway."

"Much obliged, Sylvan," the Roundman purred.

"Now, you'll tell me how you were in a position to hear this in the first place. We'll continue along this manner if you wish to learn more."

"Sounds more than fair. I used to hear it at Destaing and l'Église Street. Hear it humming out from the Champ de Mars."

"That's Serge's handiwork again. A page out of his louse book if I recall correctly."

"I didn't piece the connection that it had anything to do with the Sous until I saw children singing it in the street playing *jeu du loup*. Those same children would sell me my guavas."

I began to have one of my daydreams at the mention of the guavas. There was no bridge, however, to my life with my parents and the Royal Academy of Famous Sods and Actors in Knebsalla. My thoughts slid into uncharted waters. Vivified before me instead was my father bubbling out of the gouache brushstrokes depicting Ramgoolam's stolid forbearance – were they the same person? The flat finish took on a gauzy shimmering, like particles in asphalt coming alive with light; in this way, it was as if a flame were erupting out of his eyes and nostrils, depending on what angle I looked at it. The visage took on the qualities of stained glass, bursting with movement.

I picked up a photograph of my father from the Roundman's cache, and held it out to where the painting was, matching the edges. It wavered in my fingers and Serge's spectral figure touched down on the floor like a flicked-off eiderdown during a fit of nightmares, so effortlessly did he take to his corporeality. He was bedecked in Devoré velvet cut into a tailored suit, his collar button undone to let the air in, or the heat out, and he ordered a peach pie at the bar. No one seemed to take mind of him as he twirled the hair poking out from under his hat. His eyes had the calloused texture of caked mud. "Shagalagalu" was piping in hot through the jerry-rigged speakers attached to the jukebox. I placed the photograph between the conversationalists and Serge's statuesque body seemed almost to put his arm around the Roundman and Green, who were now eating their slices of pie heartily. Serge appeared as if he were nodding in appreciation at what each man was saying, tsk-tsking at other particulars. He brought the hands of the two men together in a ritual of assent. His skin had the texture of a lenticular Jesus.

During the middle-eight coming out of the speakers, d'Arsel's portrait began to hum with tremulous activity, like his unrepresented hips were swaying in tempo in some nether dimension. I picked up another photograph and matched it with this painting, which began to sway more energetically, cutting a pendulous arc against the wall like a peephole cover with a screw loose. The painting was carving grooves against the wall as I moved the photograph further away from me, digging through the brickwork and making noises of a burrowing animal, until the picture frames' edges were ringed with a holy light from an outside world. The painting became a hatch door, the luminosity filtering inside until Malbar stepped through and took his place on the floor, kneeling down with his left arm stretched out against the floor. Did he have a tummy ache or something?

"Shoo! Shoo!" Marjorie commanded at the man who tumbled into the bar. "I told you last time, Manwell, you're not welcome here until you pick up your tab! Don't you dare make sick in here!"

My father ambled up in my left hand to where Malbar was resting in my right, and declared, "Smacked on your axis!" At which point Malbar stood to attention as if that's all it took to cure what ailed him, and the two began to cut a rug amid all the private business that needed attending at the bar, not a soul really noticing the fetching display of Manichean capers taking place along the patterns of the terrazzo floor at the tips of my outstretched hands. Feet were stomping, pirouetting nervously; arms were disentangling themselves from invisible bonds, cast off with oafish ceremony. The whole scene was only wanting the hand of God to emerge from the ceiling for the burlesque to be complete. Marjorie escorted the dancing man out of the bar with a broom in her hand. Cherelle snatched the two photographs out of my hands, waving her hands in front of my face.

"Marjorie," Sylvan said. "We'll have some of your recovered pricked wine, if you're done a-waltzing."

Er, bring on the muck-sweat then. This Lazarus trick was done by combining half an ounce of tartarized spirit of wine with the pricked plonk, and then setting it aside for a few days to improve its balance. I'd forgotten to do this when I was asked a few nights before, and Cherelle and I were now faced with an eyesore of a dilemma. I was having trouble concentrating, but still somehow found an opened bottle of port to combine with the pricked bottle as steadily as I could. I decanted the harmonized contents carefully. By the grace of a higher power, I remembered that the sour bottle in question was from the South of France, known for its unpolished tannins. I added a dash of granulated salt to be on the safe side, to bring some coarseness to its texture, hoping no one would spot the difference.

"It's a tad on the buttery side, Green," I said, making a point not to drool. "But it will go down all the better for it."

The Green and the Roundman took their glasses and returned to the other end of the bar to resume their conference of equal parts worry and excitement. They discussed Sergent mostly, while I tried to stay standing, given how terrible I was starting to feel. The Roundman beamed at being taken into Green's confidence, whereas Green seemed relieved that Michel wasn't the obstreperous bastard he could have been when he was holding so much over the gang's heads in his portfolio, notwithstanding Darlo's threatening presence during the meeting. This wasn't the Green's area of expertise, after all, but it was technically an accounting issue of missing paraphernalia, so it fell to him anyways. I was reminded of old days as they glossed over events in the *Soustyricon* on specific dates for what felt like an eternity: specifically, the theft of the Derwish's 1962 red Wandre Tri-Lam, on which he had penned the 1969 Sous classic "Dire moi ene coup (ki qualite couillion sa)." The tune had charted better than anyone expected and only two spots behind my father's celebrated torch song "Ti Zom" on the Sous Hit Parade, a monthly tabulation of singles shifted through their own distribution system, Sousse Pouce Records:

1	(3)	ROTIN BAZAR	Inaam Haq
2	(2)	OLD FAITHFUL	Doctor of Old School
3	(-)	CHAMAREL	Stegosaur Gang
4	(1)	TI ZOM	Grand Menteur
5	(4)	CAPAVE CROIRE MO CODEX	Blue Star
6	(5)	DIRE MOI ENE COUP (KI QUALITE COUILLION SA)	Black Derwish
7	(7)	MO POU ALLE GRIS GRIS	Silver Tent Gang
8	(6)	PISTACHE POURRI	Sintok
9	(11)	TI MOMENT	Ti Pete
10	(9)	GROS BOUDOUF, GROS BOYO	Gros Boudouf
11	(10)	BOUSSE TO LIKI	Aux Contraires
12	(15)	SATURDAY NIGHT SYPHILIS	The Batchwhips
13	(-)	GUELARD	The Tollivers
14	(20)	MOUSSE TO NEZNEZ	Pourri & the Potpans
15	(12)	CARAILLE CHAUD	Teen Torpor
16	(17)	PERSONALIZE	Personality
17	(13)	SOUS MEETING MINUTES FALL 1965	Sous Gang
18	(14)	BOURIQUE	Crosscuss Gang

Darlo noticed that I was glued to the documents scattered along the bar, trying to read them from upside down. He placed his hand at the centre of the hit parade so that his palm was hovering a few inches over the clipping, then rotated it that I could see better. He gave me a silent nod of approval, as he pointed to chart position seventeen with a tapping finger. As I was reading through these details of Serge's life, of which I previously knew nothing, the Roundman caught on to my immersion. I was scanning over announcements alerting changes in secret handshakes, giving fair warning against narcs who were using outdated variations of finger curling; agony aunt columns written to Pourri in which he dished out unhelpful advice concerning where to best conceal contraband; and a weekly list of the best crimes perpetrated per season, graded along categories of their bouquet, body, balance, and finish.

"Mind yourself," the Roundman said harshly, slamming his fist over the documents. "Ca c ene discussion bien confidentiel. Or don't you know the difference?"

"There's something off about these song titles," I muttered half to myself.

"Yes, and you would know. Your English has come along

considerably since we started."

"No, this is the first I've ever heard anything about them."

"Then shut your trap."

Darlo and Green exchanged a knowing look between themselves, but made no effort to come to my defence otherwise.

"Where's the washroom?" the Roundman asked, zipping his head around like a vulture.

"It's members only," Marjorie said looking sensitively at me. "You'll have to take it outside . . . somewhere inconvenient. *Like behind a tree.*"

The Roundman stepped out grumpily, collecting his portfolio in his teeth again, and making loud bumps on the floor with his sticks. Darlo ordered another drink, while the Green lit a cigarette.

"You know your father don't want you here, 'Roundelay,'" the Green said. "He wanted you to find work outside of the Sous. He was adamant."

"I know that," I said. "But he's long gone and not here to tell me that to my face."

"He has his reasons for not wanting you here. He wants something better for you and knows the Derwish is not going to give you up so easily."

"What does that mean?"

"Cherelle can't handle the rough stuff like you. You're hairy at the heel. *His* words, not mine."

"You're some messenger."

"Yes, but don't you like a challenge? There is a certain charm to this tucked-away little dive . . ."

It had taken time, but I had finally managed to escape the grip of fascination with these villainous dunderheads. My time at the Kadadac had spared me from any interaction with the Sous, but now they came back into my life with a roaring, soaring vengeance, spurred on by their need to meet the Roundman on neutral territory. The Green stirred some baseborn sentiment within me, molded it into a solicitude I was wont to dole out in meaty proportions. I had listened to the Roundman as he bestowed on my father the dignity demanded of a diplomat; Serge became a veritable *Man of the Moment* delegate accompanied with an ontological whisper of the cosmos, which touched on my own incipient affinities in an odd way. I couldn't help but feel pity for this pathetic todger though, who lapped up everything the Sous had lied through their teeth to make into reality, while also at the same time appreciating its erstwhile effects on myself. Sergent this, Sergent that – the Roundman sounded more like his old woman than the president of his fan club.

The interloper returned in much the same fashion as when he first entered the bar, drawing us into the catastrophe of his movements with no better understanding if he had been able to relieve himself. This time he sauntered in with only a single walking stick. If anyone else noticed, they said nothing. The Roundman unlatched his portfolio open again, but made sure to use his arms to obscure my view of the documents, forming a ring around the edges of his papers, his middle and ring fingers of both hands clasping tightly, but leaving an opening for the Green to see if he did not slouch.

"Hey, Roundman," I called, picking up on Darlo's cue. "Your song titles are a bust. There were no Sous minutes in the fall of 1965. Out of respect. Death in the family."

"What? I have no idea what you're talking about. I haven't even seen that clipping in detail," the Roundman countered.

"Which one is it?" Marjorie put it to him.

"It's a clipping. I didn't make the clipping, or what was put on there. I just have the clipping. Ask the clipping, don't ask me."

The Green made a whistling sound through his nostrils that sounded like a pneumatic dentist's drill. Darlo stood up and produced a garotte made of a miniaturized volute spring he'd pinched from a garage somewhere. The garotte was quietly placed on the bar over all the artifacts laid on the table.

"Do you know what that is?" the Green asked. "Use your imagination."

The Roundman could not think of anything to say except for this hollow-sounding gargling. He had become a gargarism, if you will.

"Speak up."

Marjorie picked up a butcher's cleaver. I found in my hand a corkscrew that I had shakily made a fist around. The Green pulled out the same notebook he had fiddled with earlier and leafed through the pages. He flexed the spine of the book repeatedly, and placed it flat in front of the Roundman.

"I want you to think about how you answer this next question very carefully. Why does it say we released a cut

94

of our minutes in the fall of '65 if there were no minutes to be taken at a meeting that never happened officially? How would you know about that? Is the clipping a fabrication meant to draw us out? What's your affiliation? Because normally, we'd just have the Derwish's daughter over there slip you a few sugarlumps before dropping you off for a nighttime stroll by the McQuesten Bridge. We wouldn't even bother with asking."

I cut Cherelle a contaminated look of a double-cross at the mention of her drink-lacing on command.

The Roundman shuddered to look at me. His mouth overproduced saliva, bubbling out over his lips, impeding his ability to speak. He placed a soiled hanky over his mouth to dry its fetid corners.

"L-listen Green, the Derwish's daughter. I have no idea, none at all. You produced the hit list, maybe someone within your r-ranks would know more. What do you want from me to believe me? What do I have to do?"

The Roundman became agitated and inexplicably began removing his clothes. He started by unfastening his tie, then unbuttoning his collar. He tore at his belt and threw it at the back of the bar, where it knocked a few glasses over. He kicked off his pants, which got caught on one of his ankles. Somehow, defying the very basic laws of physics, he then went on to remove his underwear without moving from his stationary position atop one of the barstools. Imaginary children went home weeping at the sight. I gagged uncontrollably. Then I began to laugh hysterically. I could not contain myself. Looking at this naked man prostrate himself in a desperate gamble for his life was suddenly much too much, much too much for me to handle.

"My goodness, you're eager," the Green joked. "Eager as a dormouse. Ha ha ha ha! Which is a good thing. You present a unique opportunity to us, believe me? Your knowledge of rulings of exemption for one. Does it extend to those of this country? I should hope it does."

"Let's welcome the next contestant on 'Die for Nothing!'" I hollered.

"Hush you!" Darlo exclaimed. He was huddled over some papers scratching away and just barely took his eyes off his work to address me.

The Roundman began to weep into his hands, sobbing and sniffing like a whipped poodle.

"We mean to do well by your wits," Green continued. "Good, you understand me. Smashing, in fact. A little bird told us that some religions are free to renovate properties with little to no interference in this country, taxation being minimal in other respects as well. We'll start there. That's what we have an eye towards. We'll need a solicitor for that. We want to expand our operations, starting with the Kadadac. Make a hostel for weary travellers, a stop along the way. In exchange for your services, you can meet the Menteur himself. You'd like that, wouldn't you? He'll do birthday parties, you know. Now then, Michel, doesn't that sound nice? What do you say?"

"Wwaaaaah," the Roundman assented.

"I'm so pleased we've come to an agreement!" the Green said, clasping his hands demonstratively. "You must have some ideas about how to build this on up yourself. We have our own as well. Here are some stories we'd like to build this new venture around, a hagiography of the Sous. And look, with matching lobby cards! Can you see our names in lights? We can."

"Whatever you want, whatever you . . . Just for the love of God, and merciful Jesus, let me leave in one piece. Please, I don't know what you think I've done . . . or will do. But I will work to your guiding hand, this much I can promise." The Roundman tightened a grip around the Green's wrist. The Green gave a brief yelp and pulled his hand away.

"A whelp-hunting we will go, a whelp-hunting we will go," I sung to myself.

"Here, Michel," Darlo interposed, putting away his pen in his breast pocket. "Tell me what you think of this mock-up. Nothing set in stone."

Darlo handed out the lobby cards he'd hastily designed. The Roundman wept bitter tears over the caricatures of his "heroes."

It was a spectacle to see the Green and Darlo go to work. They were an efficient pair, a marvel to watch rain violence from the clouds as if it was a passing system moving through a jerkwater town. Green began a rain dance with one leg in the air to distract the Roundman's attention, while Darlo knocked the gawping fool a firebolt on his chin while he was still half-engrossed with the documents before him. Mr. Records didn't see it coming. He toppled over his stool on to the ground, taking a few drinks and his walker down with him. I leaned over the bar to see if he had broken anything. He stared dumbfoundedly into the ceiling. I threw some limes onto his forehead to see if he was conscious. He picked himself up off the ground and struggled to regain his footing, resting his arm on a low-backed stool.

"Go on, you can squeeze in a left hook if you're quick." Darlo looked to me imploringly.

"Go on," the Green said. "It's tradition around these parts."

I raised my fist in the air over my head and the Roundman's enfeebled eyes stared at me over the edge of the bar, the rest of his face obscured behind it. I let my fist drop at my side.

"He's already assented. No need to belabour it."

Marjorie helped the man up, putting some ice on a napkin for him. Staunching a trickle of blood from his nose with his index finger held horizontally beneath it, he looked at the Green with an abject look of retrenchment.

"Okay, I might know something about the hit parade."

"Oh?" the Green said in delighted surprise. "There's actually something to know?"

"Your ledger book, it has this week's tabulations?"

"So?"

"I'll show you how it works."

The Green folded back the book in half so that the Roundman could only see the one page facing him. The bleeding Pudding Pop currently passing for the Roundman took one of the Green's pens and began superscripting the latest tabulation with arrows and numbers, decoding its arcana of humble words.

The Roundman went on to explain how the chart positions from the current and previous weeks formed a date. For example, a placement of five this week represented the month of the year, and the placement in last week's list referred to the day, say the twenty-third. To complicate things further, the hit list was also designed to tip off readers in the know when a song was in motion. Only songs preceded by an uncharted song (-) the previous week were in play. The itchy bang "Mousse to Neznez," a song about cocaine consumption, was then in motion at position 14; most likely a shipment of drugs had arrived. And so forth in greater complication.

"Who's running this? This is off the books if it's the first I'm hearing of it."

"Who do you think? Who's in charge of all your contraband? Or I should say *was* before Pourri took over."

"Let's get back to the Sous minutes. Quickly, quickly! Tell me what you know so we can stop the bombarbinating gibberish in my skull."

"Did you release any wax the week of those minutes? I'm assuming minutes were taken, if not released outright."

"Don't look at meee," I remarked. "I was there, but Cherelle's the one that did all the note-takinguh."

Darlo and the Green rushed to confer with Cherelle, I assumed over how this nobody could call them on their bluff as if a recording of the Sous minutes of 1965 were the real McCoy.

The Roundman and I were left alone at the end of the bar closest to the kitchen.

"Has the Green given you the money?" the Roundman asked slyly.

I made no reply.

"Hey, sourpuss. I'm talking to you. Has the Green given you the money or hasn't he?"

"What money would that beeee?" I giggled through the asking, surprised at the sound of my own voice.

"Pfft. Typical. The Green's not to be trusted. You're coming with me."

"Who are youuu again? Do I know youuu?"

"Listen to me, they've given you *something*. To soften you up for my thrashing. Don't you know an initiation when you see one? You're not thinking straight. Your father sent me."

"Whassafahzer?"

"Stop messing about, we don't have much time. You haven't given them the codex, have you?"

"I'll sell youuu the codexex. Add to youuur quooolection. $500, cheeeap."

"You're right, that is cheap for what you stand to make from the information inside. Listen to me, your father gave you a right good bashing before the Blue Boar meeting. Malbar revealed the location of the mantelet in the hit parade – that's what you saw Serge throw into the fire. Serge said you would trust me if I told you this."

I started to claw at my face and make mushy sounds out of my cheeks. Nausea crept up from the pit of my stomach where it was hiding. The room was starting to spin.

"Seeeeerrrrrrrzzzzzuuuuh," I squalled.

"It's ego-dissolution, but it's temporary. It's going to wear off in a few hours. Just remind yourself that. Listen to the sound of my voice. Your father doesn't want you working here or anywhere near here. I'm going to make a run for it. If you can meet me at Dundurn Castle in ninety minutes, I'll be waiting for you in an orange Corvair Rampside. It's a truck, running board on the driver's side. I can't wait very long, and Serge will consider our debt paid as long as I make a go of saving you. In case you forget, I've written it down for you."

The Roundman stiffened and collected his walking stick. He weighed it in his palm, then decided to grip it with both hands for better manoeuvrability. I realized then that there was nothing wrong with his legs after all. He placed the stick on top of the bar, holding it by its handle. I saw the hair rise from the nape of his neck. Exhaling, the Roundman's legs tensed, and then exploded forward like an uncoiled spring. He put his weight against the bar, and using the angle of his leaning body for leverage, proceeded to collect all the assorted glassware, earthenware, shakers, condiments, and cutlery in the momentum of his strides. Broken crockery splashed everywhere and made a terrible din which reverberated across the room. As he dragged these items towards the entrance, the Roundman occasionally gave a flick of his wrist so that alternately, some of his passengers were left behind him, and other pieces were flung in the direction of everyone at the bar. A shot glass struck Darlo clear between the eyes while he was dolloping heaps of Crisco into his mouth from the tin. Cherelle had time to cover her face just in time for a mug to hit her. The Green ducked and had horseradish and chimichurri pour over his new hat in thick, gelatinous drips.

"I thought you searched him, you half-wit!" the Green protested. "Love a duck, he's firing those steel-jackets like he means it!"

Cherelle slumped down beside her uncle and rubbed her temples, making no answer. I heard the kitchen door beside me and saw it gently move open an inch or two, before falling back silently. The Roundman campaigned for the Green's notebook and jacket at the edge of the bar with his fingers. He nearly missed them, but emerged triumphantly at the main entrance. With one foot already halfway through the door, he paused, then stepped back inside. "He's going to lob something at Darlo for that slap," I thought to myself. Darlo poked his head up and was clouted with a salt shaker-cum-torpedo in the neck. The Roundman then pulled a lever somewhere from his walking stick, exposing a naked blade at the verticillate base where the four legs converged. He pulled another tab and the legs fell away. Bérenger next. It would have to be. Pulling the javelin well behind his waist, the Roundman leaned into his throw and lobbed it underhandedly at a forty-five degree angle into the air, where it tore through the Bérenger painting and landed somewhere by the rail, taking a bottle of gin with it. The painting depicted the politician with his arms akimbo in a posture of conquest; it now more accurately looked as if Bérenger was repeatedly picking his nose, the gash beginning at his left elbow and moving across his torso to rest at the tip of his nostril. The sound of ". . . and you throw a punch like a moose squibs a fart!" echoed off along with the sounds of the Roundman's dynamic exit.

Then, a few real shots broke out and I saw little puffs of smoke come out from behind the bar. Someone was shooting a Manurhin revolver wildly into the air and mostly straight into the apartment above, though a bullet went so far as to puncture the jukebox, putting an end to our Mick Rowley danger music.

"I've been bloody poisoned! Lordy my stomach feels like mince and tatties!" the Green moaned histrionically.

Marjorie came blaring out of the kitchen like her hair was on fire, and let loose with a double-barrelled shotgun at the entrance door. The recoil sent her flying back through the kitchen. By this point I too had adopted the nuclear position below a table along with the other patrons. All the sounds were louder and more vivid than they should have been and gave a pulsing, paranoid dimension to my thoughts. Waves of fear pressed down from the tip of my head, which gave me the sense of being flattened inside a box.

When the madness was all over, and people started picking themselves up from the floor, I could tell that it was a good thing that we were tasked by Marjorie so soon afterwards with work, for it unjangled the rattling in my fingers and gave me a sense of calm. Cherelle and I had the place looking somewhat presentable only an hour later. The glass had been broomed to one corner of the Kadadac, making a beautiful pyramid of fractured colour. The bar had been wiped down perfunctorily, the patrons told to leave. The Green, however, was the only one left in a state. I had never seen him so out of sorts, fretting over the consequences.

"I should have stayed with Serge, I should have stayed with Serge . . ." he kept repeating.

Marjorie dismissed Cherelle and me early. Cherelle was uncomfortable walking with me, but what choice did she really have? No one had bothered to tell her where she'd be staying while she worked the Kadadac, and I guess it fell to me to fill in the blanks of the arrangement with Marjorie. I was probably leading us around in circles, but my poisoner still followed as my shadow. I was still in such a way that I couldn't be bothered to send her packing even if I wanted to and even as she kept demanding where I was taking her.

The more I dwelled on it, the more it seemed everything had transpired as if I were influencing the bones of reality; that was the impression I was left with. Was this what it felt like to be my father? For everything I wanted to happen did happen. Even my conversation with Cherelle took this strange, theopneust quality. I felt like I could predict her responses before she made them. Perhaps in this way we were closer than I had initially thought. So I cut her some slack. No one ever did. I had to remember that, unlike Christian, and to a far lesser degree, Annaleigh, there were no judgments with Cherelle, even if her actions betokened a coarser understanding of friendship. This counted for something in my books.

The effects of whatever I had ingested were wearing off, and I could feel the cloudiness of my thoughts resume a shame-imperilled lucidity. The world had lost its jarring newness. All that was left was the slinking of time, locking and unlocking before us.

We were turning on to Barton from MacNab Street North, a few blocks east of Dundurn Castle, when we saw an orange Corvair turned halfway onto the curb in a starfish sprawl of clawed-in dirt and skid marks. I followed the truck's tracks with my eyes around one of the street corners, which came from the direction of the Kadadac. The driver's door was open, and someone's head was between their legs, while a woman on the running board pulled his hair back for him. There was the awful sound of retching going on. The birds were even keeping their distance. My curiosity drew me headlong into the scene, where I could almost imagine the *Hinterland Who's Who* music playing in between my ears.

Myself: Is that you in there, Round Round Roundman?

Marjorie: Why didn't you come alone?

Myself: What are you doing here!?

Marjorie: I'm here because you can't follow instructions!

Cherelle: What's wrong with him?

Marjorie: He's got it as bad as the Green does. What did you serve?

Myself: Nothing. Just what Green asked.

Marjorie: Did I ask you to pour a half bottle of port in with pricked wine?

Cherelle: I don't have to be here.

Marjorie: Stop being such a wallflower, Cherelle. You're obviously not wanted, but we can't very well send you away until we can make sure you can keep your yap closed.

Roundman: Ugh . . . You came. Good. Get blurgh . . .
    Get in.
Myself: Wasn't born yesterday.
Marjorie: You've got two of us now telling you he's on
    the level. Get in the truck. Give her the letter.
Myself: Letter?

TI AIGRE DOUX. GREEN WENT TO HIGHEST BIDDER.
TOUGH ON ME. NO REASON FOR THE SAME TO YOU.
FUCK HIM. MICHEL SPEAKS TRUE. MARJORIE CAN BE
TRUSTED. BOTH FROM THE CROSSCUSS GANG. JUST
    DETAILS . . . YOU WILL SEE CHAPEL BELLS SOON.
NOTHING ELSE EXPECTED, BEYOND ATTENDANCE.
FOR PERMANENCE'S SAKE, **LISTEN TO ME FOR ONCE**.
GET OUT WHILE GETTING GOOD. DERWISH WANTS
YOU FOR NEW VIDEUR OR MENACEUR. WON'T BE
PRETTY. BAD PROSPECTS. ASK POURRI. THE WORLD
    IS A HANGING PLACE. SAUVER COT CAPAV.

—AN ELEPHANT WITHOUT HIS ANT

Myself: That's it?
Marjorie: *C'est tout.*
Myself: When's he coming to get me?
Marjorie: . . .
Roundman: What about her?
Marjorie: Cherelle, mind me carefully. You can either
    come back with me, or we're going to leave you
    strung up against that tree with your wits the only

thing standing between you freezing yourself to sleep.

Cherelle: I'll keep quiet.

Marjorie: Lord knows you've done enough tonight. How much did you give her?

Cherelle: Just a handful . . .

Marjorie: Cherelle, go stand by that tree over there.

Roundman: You better get back, Marjie-bird. Here, I have what the Menteur wanted.

Myself: How are you going to get that back to the Green without him noticing?

Marjorie: If he's noticed that it's gone, I'll put the ledger in the pile of glass you swept up earlier. If not, then it's not up for discussion.

Roundman: Thanks for not blowing my head off.

Marjorie: You don't need my help for that.

Myself: What did you skim from the book?

Roundman: Your father doesn't get updates because he's abroad. That's one. Our game of cricket will remind Tweedledeetwit and Tweedledumtwat that just 'cause the cat's away, doesn't mean the mice can play. That's two. Don't look so proud, Cherelle. If you know something, believe me, it's by the grace of Serge that you do. Go further back!

Marjorie: Call me if something comes up.

Roundman: You only need to keep the Derwish's girl quiet until we make it out of town. If the Derwish gives you trouble after, which he's liable to do once she sings, you can tell him to forget the deal with

his pamphlets and his student exchanges. That
should smooth out your ride for the time being.

The Corvair kicked up a mean spray of dust and debris out
over the distance where Cherelle and Marjorie receded
into vanishing points. I leaned my head out the window
and made sure to scream loud enough so that Cherelle
could hear me: "This means we're even now!" I could just
make out Marjorie walloping Cherelle across the face with
her pinochle-seasoned hands. We headed west for a short
spell, then curved northeast sharply with the girdling of
the lake by the motorway. The Roundman turned down
the radio and handed me a jar of pickled *palmistes*.

"That's all I could scrape by for dinner. I'm sorry. I'm
not risking that with where my stomach is sitting at the
moment. Far cry from my youth, but that's life."

"How did you meet Serge? I never seen you before."

"Beau Bassin. Was holed up in there at one of them
clinics a while back now, for polio."

"Where are you taking me, Roundman? Where is my
father?"

"We've got a date with God, like the letter said. You'll
take my name. When we're done there, I'll give you the
value of the money Green was skimming from your pay.
We'll set you up with your own flat, which you'll have to
sort out for yourself on your own later, and then you will
do what your father said to do in the first place: You'll find
work, and you'll make your way and you'll make it stick.
Like the rest of us."

"I'm not seeing the silver lining."

"Not that anyone ever does."

I wanted next to ask the Roundman why he had stripped his clothes in the bar. Of the many things that did not make immediate sense to me in the past few hours, this stood out as being the most ill-advised. Then I started to ask myself whether I had hallucinated the entire thing, if such a thing was even possible given what I had eaten. Without any kind of verbal prompting though, Michel started in by saying, "Do you know the legend of Pillywick? He's a Piltdown Man sort of figure. He would show up at your door wearing a trench coat, stride through, and peel the outer skin away to reveal his naked body before bludgeoning you to death. The Sous have nightmares about his Crosscuss shadow-companion, Hunspach: a killer who will arrive to your doorstep naked, step through, do your head in, and leave with your clothes on his back. If you ever saw a naked man or the sartorial twin of someone you knew walking down the boulevard, you'd do well to keep clear of him. The Green will catch on, when he goes through today's events in his head over and over again. That's what he does; all an accountant is ever good for. Add to the mix that he's superstitious as a Pamplemousses washwoman, and you have established some distance between him and the Derwish. Green gets to be too bold when he's aligned with his brother-in-law for too long. Are you listening? Try to learn something for a change that isn't in one of your damn books. You can only buy the Green's loyalty for so long. The same is true for everyone. Keep that in mind the next time you stick something foreign in your mouth you don't know where it come from. Don't get mixed up with the Derwishes. If you do, know when to take them into your confidence, and when to show them the back side of your hand. Your dad, on the other hand, has done right by us, maintaining good relations. He's the only one of you lot we are happy to deal with. Again, not like Derwish, who wants a finger in every pie. I would reckon if there was anyone you'd want to dismantle the whole operation, it'd be his head on a platter you'd be wanting."

How was this for expositional service? Clearly the Crosscussers liked their movies as much as the Sous did. They all sounded like George Raft half the time talking. The truck chugged along the motorway, pushing along at a steady clip. The Roundman kept quiet and his hands to himself for the rest of the ride. I held some contrary opinions in my mind – the care and attention my father took in procuring Malbar's possessions and arranging his mock-burial at our home, the distance he put between us while also showing me, through Michel, a guiding hand of paternal responsibility at one foul stroke if at a far remove.

Was this the spilling-over point of our relationship, when with disgust I saw how much tenderness he showed Malbar and how little he had in reserve for me? He gave me away to Michel without the slightest touch of humanity. In like fashion, Michel gave me away to myself, where I could trace my trajectories as a spent and traded object. I paid for Serge's guilt, I cleared away Michel's debt, I was the equity on the Derwish's new Grand Videur, and the creditor of some kind of bizarre collateral from dead Malbar. All in a day's work or not, I was picking up some spectacularly loathsome baggage and needed a way to jettison it into the unconscious.

While I was rooting around in the mind's mental garbage cluster for extra space, I knew that dinner was waiting for me: roast partridge by the whiff of it. I could see old mum was out digging the garden, while Serge was just putting the final touches to his memoirs, *Grand Menteur*, from his angel's roost of a study. Outside my bedroom windows, I could see the lintel and the branches that swooped across it were covered with rime, a happy portent for the period of rejuvenation that followed thereafter. Serge and Virma would later have a terribly awful row about it, but they would soon know it for the best, my first year away from the nest at Imperial College. I would come back a better person, more resilient than before. The comely city and its happy perversions were to be mine again. And as it should be.

8.

Soustyricon Late Edition. Saturday, March 23rd, MCMLXXIV

Credo: *To cast accounts with impunity, to roll loaded dice behind animated whistling, and to engineer the perils of a thousand thundercracks lashing the earth's hide from the penumbral distance*

Bullet-studded brouhaha in Sous-protected Kadadac bar

HAMILTON, ON. – In what eyewitnesses are calling a violent brush with death, prominent Sous members the Bowling Green and Darlo were marked for bitter-ends execution by persons currently unknow. The ailed assassination attempt took place at popular Mauritian watering hole the Kadadac in Hamilton's North End. Owner Marjorie Armistead was on hand to defend her valued patrons with eight spirited salvos of her sawed-off Browning Citori. It is suspected that the assailant – rumoured to be Hunspach, the Crosscuss Gang's resident psycho-killer – sustained wounds to the stomac in his getaway, though the suspect still remains at large.

"I don't doubt it was him," Green, the Sous' Grand Comptable, said to *Soustyricon* cub reporter Piom Namboothiri by telephone. "No one knows what he looks like for on thing, but he stripped before us. Unprovoked, before making of with my jacket. Then the nextthing we knew, a hail of righteous bullets rained down on us. Only by the good graces of my Sous rupee was I protected from harm, that I can be sure of. I clung to it like my life depended on it, which it wholly did."

Crosscuss leaders have long denied inolvement with the vehemence of Hunspach's international actions. "He's a loose cannon, ca betasse," Crosscuss spokesperson Quel Tapaze stated emphatical. "You can't even point him in the right direction. We may have given that hellhound an agency of purpose, but he's no association with us for five years this coming summer."

Speculation has been rampant about what political consequences between the gangs might result in the wake of these events, especially in view of the Joint Enrolment campaign proposed earlier this year, which would allow junior members of the groups to enrol in seminars taught by their counterparts.

"No, I don't think this will have any bearing on the Program," the Green averred when pressed for comment. "I'm friendlywith Comptroller Sakibonsa, and we're in agreement that the exchange of our youth will enrich our respective causes. The Sous don't endorse the Crosscussers' broader project, but we respect it."

Possible motives for the hit are at the time of publication slim. Sous insiders who spoke on the condition of anonymnymity suggested the Kadadac was to have been the locale of a new business venture that would revolutionize Sous activity on that continent with "a supercharged view to expansion."

It has also been suggested that doubt is currently being fanned in the inner chambers of Sous upper command against the Green's ability to perorm his stipulate duties. Reports from competing media suggest a loss of confidence in someone who could walk so isastrously into a trap. "How can the bloke you have running the numbers so stupidly be caught unaware when his number was up? I'm bafled that this is the person we have playing with the purse strings of our monies," one Sous member remarked in a privatesetting of confidentiality. *Con'd on A7*

Menteur's new single a swing and a miss

"Fourmi" (Mayacou) – Unreleased studio outtake from 1974 OUTBREAK recording sessions, given official release this week on the chart-topping, career-spanning compilation LP, IN BED WITH AN INBRED, and serving as Grand Menteur's 52nd single. A rare turn to dripping sentimentalism, the song features the pouting lips of a theo-

rbo ensemble interlude and cops to an "I Melt Like Butter" on diarrhea riff that can be sussed from a mile away. The narrator laments the abandonment of a loved one with shocking, overblown bravura; listeners are dragged by hook or crook through the gullied backwater of the singer's guilt. Aficionados will undoubtedly be a cross-breed of confusion and disgust over this toxic about-face of the Menteur's coveted talents. One can sniff the funk of an autobiographical strain behind this objectively bad piece of fluff that would make the Lyke-Wake Dirge sound like a Des Champ number. Carried over like the oddments of old ideas, it is hard to see what secret import its aperçus may hold for learned readers in the know (<u>please contact this publication if you can provide further insight on this basis for a nominal reward</u>). – Bowling Green
More reviews in Arts & Life

Sous members sanctified in local theatre with lobby cards

Name: Kaartikeya Derwish

AKA: Black Derwish, The Spinning Death, Vice-Dictator

Sous Classification: Grand Piqûre

Affiliation: Sous Gang, Mayasous & Sons Leather Company, Alimo's Produce

Rank: Fructuarius

Cover: Costermonger

Claim to Fame: Sold kidney stones as high-end imported dates

Slugging Percentage: .6901

Acta Sanctorum: Ability to unripen ripened fruit

Name: Serge Mayacou
AKA: Sergent, The Great Pause, Undulating Vibration of Hate
Sous Classification: Grand Menteur
Affiliation: Sous Gang, Mayasous & Sons Leather Company
Rank: Mendax
Cover: Consultant
Claim to Fame: Too many to mention
Slugging Percentage: .7090
Acta Sanctorum: ~~Lied his way into existence.~~ Revived dead chicken by
blowing on it

Name: Syneo Pasquas
AKA: Ti Pourri, Small Rotten, Poop Picture, Corona Nose, Human
Expectorate, the Father of Noble Gases
Sous Classification: Grand Videur
Affiliation: Sous Gang, Mayasous & Sons Leather Company
Rank: Interfector
Cover: Lion-Tamer
Claim to Fame: Only gang member to have successfully petitioned for
membership after expulsion
Slugging Percentage: .7293
Acta Sanctorum: The subject of numerous plagues and diseases while in
exile from Sous

Name: Sylvan Yarlet Lachman
AKA: The Bowling Green, Yarlet the Varlet, Beanie
Sous Classification: Grand Comptable
Affiliation: Sous Gang, Mayasous & Sons Leather Company

Rank: Computare
Cover: Farrier
Claim to Fame: Can settle any books given unlimited resources and
unlimited time
Slugging Percentage: .6624
Acta Sanctorum: Was impervious to all abortifacients while inside
mother's womb

Name: Alain Renaux
AKA: Malbar, Old Faithful, Prolapse Breath
Sous Classification: Grand Itinérant
Affiliation: Sous Gang, Mauritian Police Force (Vice Squad)
Rank: Languidulus
Cover: Bon Vivant/Charity Case
Claim to Fame: Has pledged over 687 immigration applications for
"relatives"
Slugging Percentage: .5922
Acta Sanctorum: Incorruptibility

Name: Quirinal Favrod
AKA: Darlo, Loverling, Sauvage, Mary Oddfellows
Sous Classification: Grand Menaceur
Affiliation: Sous Gang
Rank: Perturbatrix
Cover: Stablehand
Claim to Fame: Once consumed an entire bottle of surfactants on a bet
Slugging Percentage: .4321
Acta Sanctorum: Pending verification

Glossary of crime – *Week of March 22nd, 1974.*

<u>Kadadac Incident</u>: Attempted assassination attempt of Sous members the Bowling Green and Darlo
Bouquet: Smoky with notes of vengeance
Body: Medium-build, perhaps using a walking stick
Balance: Uneven to a fault, with the bold, honeyed flavours of viciousness being undercut by the disappointment of failure and the maladroitness of bad aim
Finish: Bitter, with poor purity and no style

<u>Sausy Man French</u>: Arrest of Serge Mayacou by local police forces in Belgium, while carrying 80 lbs of Mauritian sausage in the form of chainmail
Bouquet: Briny with hints of cumin and quince
Body: Voluptuously heavy, for the season
Balance: Harmonious, a headlong voyage into the minerality of an arrest, and onwards through the herbaceousness of salvation
Finish: A versatile end one can revel in, as a master of the craft turns a confiscation into a new and steady consumer base of Belgian police – flawless and highly recommended

<u>The Poule Bouilli Encounter</u>: Receipt of stolen artworks by unknown artist portraying pushcart poulterer in the nude
Bouquet: Positively absurd – aromas of pencil lead, leather, and guava compote
Body: Not something we are likely to remember
Balance: Beyond the pale (of comparison)

Finish: A fiery end never to be mentioned again
Con'd on B3

Purgative alouda recipe claims top prize at Vittlesous festival

Ingredients:
- – 1 litre of milk (whole milk preferably)
- – 500 ml of water
- – 2–3 tablespoons of soaked basil seeds (tukmaria)
- – 1 stick of agar agar (alternately one can of grass jelly)
- – strawberry syrup (add to taste)
- – sugar (optional)
- – rum (optional)

Method: Combine ingredients, shake well, and refrigerate before serving. Drink is a purgative: don't say I didn't warn you! *Con'd on C3*

Letters to the editor

Q: What is wrong with your letterpress type blocks? You are always missing "d" and "f" in your news articles.
A: uck o
Q: I know something you don't know.
A: So do your mother and I.
Q: I have seen the gablou in possession of this paper. You may want to alternate your distribution cycle/routes.
A: Noted.
Q: I miss the Sous Fables you used to print. Are there any further plans for pushcart poulterer adventures?

A: None at the moment. We are honouring the poulterer's memory by finding those responsible for the **Poule Bouilli Encounter**. *Con'd on E6*

Sous/Crosscuss mneumonic recruitment pamphlet a historic co-venture in gang activity

RIPAILLES, MAURITIUS – Updates to the Sous and Crosscuss Gangs' recruitment protocols are taking effect immediately following recent evelopments in cross-border regulation in the Americas. In an effort to stem the tide of eclines in onations (historically originating from the hands of aging members), the Black Derwish has called for a restructuring of enrollment practices to curtail the alarming trend.

"People die and don't take the necessary precautions in ensuring the generation following has a sense of where they come from, and how they come to certain knowledge bases. It's a travesty," the Vice-Dictator said.

The new updates would clariy Sous and Crosscuss positions on key political issues, while at the same time, improve upon notional areas of gang philosophy.

"The problem is isolating exactly when a Sous or Crosscusser feels alienated from his brotherhood and sisterhood," Derwish elaborated. "Once this perio in time is localized, we can surgically eliminate the objectionable thought cascades to our advantage, ensuring the esirable outcomes in thinking. Those in charge of enrolment, even our front-line members, are urged to use this mnemonic to identify potential canidates for consideration."

When met with the accusation that Derwish was brainwashing impressionable minds, regardless of their age groups, he responded, "I don't think you're inflecting that statement with enough congratulatory vigour."

Though exact numbers could not be accessed determining exact losses or gains in registration, not everyone shares the Derwish's dour outlook.

Piom Namboothiri, cub reporter for the *Soustyricon* on loan from the Crosscussers as part of the Joint Enrolment Program test phase, is an expert on gang dynamics. "The Derwish don't understand capital goods. Gang members rarely opt out of this life wholesale. They trade up for a newer model. And what the Sous lose, another gang stands to gain. If the Sous can manage to keep up with the other groups, they'll be rewarded for their efforts with a larger average of productivity as production forces increase. No one wants to be a Crosscusser forever neither!"

The *Soustyricon* has been given an early draft of the enrolment procedure, which charts the inception of gang potential up until acceptance. Pamphlets containing the mnemonic device will be available at locations where savvy individuals will know to find them. *Con'd on C2*

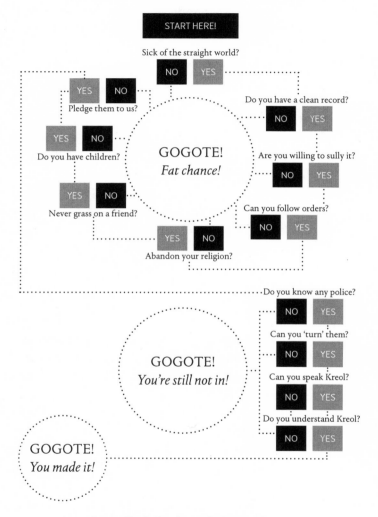

Presented by the Sous Gang & the Crosscuss Gang

9.

St. Albans Homeless Shelter, Moss Park,
Toronto, Canada, 1979

SOME STODGY-FACED COW'D found herself in the envi-
able position of deciding just how far she was willing to
challenge lavatory conventions when they radioed me
to come in after her. I'd finally got my head around some
peace and quiet in the Repair Shop, having just helped one
of the molls from Human Recourses retrieve a stapler that
was lost in the nook behind her desk – though truths be
told it may as well have been a culvert underneath Hell-
mouth I hadn't ventured there in so long a spell. The two-
way belt box they'd made standard issue squawked orders
to add haste to our travels to the women's lav, because

some grog-blossom had stumbled her way in and presently out crying foul rape and holy Christian murder, only for this time she had more than enough bog rolls to shake a stick at. I dragged my heels by making a few laps around the south stairwells, making sure not to catch any of the paths that, to my knowledge, Jake frequented: first order of business, and a good one at that.

By the time I got the main exit doors flung open, they'd of course barked a few times more, the impatient pissholes. There was a crowd forming too, with the slag who'd initially signalled for the cavalry commanding space and vigilance with her eyes, which were then half-obliged to spin into the back of her head. She had what looked like Bird's Custard thickening out the side of her jaw. The whole thing was a scene right out of *Good Housekeeping*, it was so pathetic: the one who'd identified the bronze David, reclining into the arms of what looked like a human dewlap, pardon the vividity, who was in turn sunning this ragged bag of bones back to life.

"Look who's finally decided to wake up," Adrienne, the woman supporting Custard-face, said almost confidingly. "You dirty malingerer. This is serious. You can't be taking your sweet and fabulous time every time we page you."

I ignored the insinuation, and traced my eyes from the woman lying on the floor to the lavatory doorway. I slid my hand in gently through a crack of the door, and then bent my head in to interpret the gruesome details. Almost instantly, I recoiled. Human biology be damned it smelled a foul thing.

"Pshaw! It's black as Newgate's knocker in there!" I hollered.

Though decency forbade it, science proclaimed it, and so I asked if it was true what had been reported, but the grim faces before me looking with disgust rendered these queries fantastically unnecessary; the perpetrator had retreated back into the folds of the wet slop being handed out with aggrieved entitlement, and thus the crowd around me were happy to instead refocus the impropriety in question to my having taken so long to get to this hot zone of our late assembly, human filth all present and accounted for. I had half the mind to ask them if they'd want me to set the stalls on fire. I put together the pieces of how I would tackle the problem – deck scrub, vacuum, wax it into posterity-preserving callosity – flitting through my head like a rotten picture show. On the grounds of this investigative process, I thought it perfectly within my rights to ask, "What would you lot give it on the Beaufort Scale?"

Bird's Custard, who was halfway to heel-standing with the support of two bosoms under each of her arms, swooned at my indelicate description of our female feculences. So instead, I retreated from that miserable litter of tits, assuring them I'd be back with a lead chamois, and could practically hear shoes go unroping off stockinged feet. I reached for my two-way and held it to my mouth. Now how to phrase this without arousing untoward suspicion of those listening in on that channel?

"Come in, Terrence. Terrence. Over."

"What do you want, dumpling face?" buzzed the magic stick in my hands.

"Can you answer last page? I'm off-site. En route to you. Over."

"What is it?"

"By sounds of it, you'd better bring something to digest it with. Somebody had a good bab in the sink, and a sight too much fun by the looks of it."

"Copy that."

That was the order of the day ever since I started working at the shelter – the biggest of its kind in the city and for that reason, an altar call to all the privation that frothed wildly at the margins. Vagabonds converged morning, afternoon, and night for a kip or a place to rest a tracking arm. Kitchen staff would serve lunch promptly at eleven, and then you'd have the stinking aftermaths to deal with, before having the same goings-on again after supper – always the worst after a meal. Mucous-stained hankies, plastic cutlery strewn about like lonely Billy no-mates, scag needles, sauces thick as bilge-water, upturned garbage, prophylactics on dinner plates – you name it, we'd had it. It was then only lunchtime, and knowing I'd be faced with similarly bleak prospects in just a few hours, I made no bones about asking for volunteers. No one can say I weren't a team player. To think I abandoned a future with the Sous for this poppycock . . . or rather Serge didn't deem me worthy of that life, chucking me away like a soiled hanky. For what else were Cherelle and I good for other than cleaning after others, waiting on them hand and foot? The perfect and exemplary case of futility. A mandate of impregnable servitude, of having your handicraft snuffed out without sanction, seemed fitting in a skewed way. I had little clue as to what Cherelle was presently occupying her time with, but odds were that her prospects couldn't be much better than mine.

You don't know heartache until someone sullies the reflection in the floor you've just shined to sweet and glorious perfection – five will get you ten that'll get your goat. Or say you got a table to look just right with no cock-ups; before you could say "Bingo, job well done!" someone's decided to improve the woodwork and your boss is out with his camera to swear evidence against you, damn the trouble of developing the pictures. Floors and furniture, the photo-man asks himself: "Who the rotten hell gets off on pictures of dirty tables?" If that kind of "thoughtfulness" didn't breed morosity, then you've got water on the brain, my son. I don't pretend that I'm sculpting an Ivor Lewis, but it's my work, and to have it all of a sudden scuppered is the same lash of an insult as any other, be it by pen or sacrilege, don't try to tell me otherwise.

It's a thankless service in any event, so it should come as no surprise to anyone that I'm racking my head on ways to get my own back – double, triple whatever I'm owed. I keep a log of every extra minute I put in at St. Albans and conversely, a record of how many hours I've stolen from those skull-grinding bastards. Twenty thousand two-hundred and eighty hours I've pocketed, which is one million two hundred and sixteen thousand eight hundred minutes I've managed to regain for services bloody-well rendered.

I'm not going to argue about what's right or wrong in the world when I got the boot-heel grinding down the back of my neck; you couldn't teach right and wrong if you tried (pity that do).

I'd like to tell those educated, dribbling pissholes that it was easy enough to bark orders until you were blue in the face, but if you were the ones actually bending your nose over the grindstone, you wouldn't be in such a hurry to assign such impudent means of deposition, never mind the stupid, petty busywork. It still gets me all het-up thinking about every little thing they've designed for their amusement on this island of crooked misadventure they call St. Albans.

Sometimes I like to think of what it'd be like if my colleagues carried on like they were all one of Cary Grant's pilots on Barranca Airways, ready to shave their peckers for any job, any job the Dutchman will send their way to get close to some of that heady empyrean. If they only make the right noises, then they'd soon thrill at gangdom highs. Can you imagine our bottom-feeding legion, tripping over dust mop and ratchet, clawing at each other to be the first to get at a blood clot on a toilet seat? Skipping to clogged trapways to get shoulder deep in adventure? Maybe then Jean Arthur would show them some tenderness in their cabins and reveal the secret of what it means to be a man. "They must love it," she'll cry, blubbering herself into pissing throes of deep emotion. "*Cleaning*, I mean. It's like being in love with a buzzsaw." This was my only type of confederation – the camaraderie of Terrence, Jeffries, and Van Leeuwen my only solace in dark and lonely hours. There were arguments between us, but there were no stakes, no sense of coming together for a grander design beyond unpacking supplies from the loading dock – no colour of danger and delinquency. The straight world didn't make room for that. It pleated down your folds and smoothed you out for the rank and file, constellated the world with petit-bourgeois worry and called it paradise. But it was a reliable paradise at that. You just have to know what sort of blighter you're going to be. That'll keep them from screwing you deeper into the ground. I don't need that spot of bother, the aggravation on top of the aggravation of living, and if I can add to theirs once in a while, well you can ask yourself again who's the lucky duck when you tally your final accounts.

I made myself scarce from this women's job well done, and I was reminded quite stabbingly of a few other jobs I'd been tasked to do, curse of curses. I ranked the jobs from most to least pressing in my head and then complimented my feet on carrying me to the site of the last task, because I'd spent plenty of loafing man-hours skulking about and extending the longest routes: relocate the deliveries for processing, shuffle some files in Accounting, and service the washrooms. I had learned how to arrange reality into doses that were manageable after all. I had just handled the washrooms in my own good way, so I hobbled over to Accounting where I knew some good tattle could be had. With all the work I'd expended, I deserved some sort of reprieve from the bit of gyp I'd subjected my eyes to.

Accounting and my deliverance was just a rag's-breadth

away when Jake swung around the corner in front of me, his eyes fixed on some colourful pasteboard in his hands. I considered pole-vaulting over a nearby cubicle, but remembering how only the angels had wings, I saw that the landing if nothing else would draw his attention to me, not to mention whomever I ended up flattening into chewing gum. I decided to stand still with my hands slapping the cubicle walls with a dirty rag I had in my back pocket, like pickle-faced Timothy Carey in *Rio Conchos*.

In the hollow space of remembrance which opened in my mind before Jake opened his mouth, I considered what differentiated me from my father. Because Jake was my Derwish in a sense, a constant thorn in my side, but not so easily fobbed off as an imbecile. He was a contender in his own way. But Serge wouldn't have dealt with him the way I had done. Serge remade his world according to the discipline and form of cinematic injunction, as if its physics could be overlaid our own laws of nature. I merely looked to its formidable enchantments as a footnote to progress, or barring that, however far along my life had come. Serge would have brought off Jake's elimination, whereas I had no hand of influence in that regard. Norman Wisdom was someone Serge propitiated for advancement in life; Timothy Carey, magnetic though he was, to me was little more than a haruspex's homework: I derived no fortune-favouring from Carey, only his diagnostic of my torturous existence.

"Oh," Jake said, interrupting my reverie. "There you are."

"Yes, fair cop. Nowhere for me to hide now."

"There's been an incident in the washroom that needs

looking after."

"Yes. It seems more than I can handle, so I asked Terrence to tough it out. It's more up his alley I think. Can you believe it? Some slum-bitch didn't rate two feet off the floor enough of a challenge, so she thought the sink would be more to her liking. Ha, ha, ha!"

"You know, it's not our place to regard their respective struggles unfavourably."

"Very high-minded of you. Though I suppose it's easy to say that when you're not mucking your hands in it."

"But I thought Terrence was . . ."

"I meant figuratively. Figuratively, Jake, of course. We in the Maintenance Department have our share of stories, you know? Stories that would put hair on your chest."

Talking to swankpot Jake was a bit of a gamble; on the face of it, you were almost sure to meet with a slippery kind of talk, where you hated yourself for being amidships the leaky starliner of boredom. Sometimes you'd approach him just to see how far you could go in those dithering circles to see if you did a loop back to the original article of discussion before you flounced off. I should know, not least of all because out of the four of us stalwarts in Maintenance, I'd very nearly done it. You were left with no bloody choice in fact, when you consider that a hundred dollars was at stake between us to the first of our department to do it, such was the reduced state of activity we were left to, having found no better rousing alternative to doing nothing. You had to practically invent your own adventures, what with the absence of the African sun and the misdemeanours of crime . . .

"Your hired hands are making a mess upstairs," I said, laying out the board. "Cement lain everywhere, risers blown open. Did you talk to them yet?"

"I was meaning to, but I haven't had the chance. I'll talk to Jeffries about it tonight. Maybe he'll be able to have a word." *Second move.*

"They won't listen to him, dammit. They'll lock him in the boiler room and throw away the key. It's got to be you if you want some traction."

"I'll tell them they'll have to clean up after themselves so that it won't make more work for you in the morning. I understand when you're doing that kind of back-breaking labour all night, the last thing on your mind is cleaning after yourself when you know someone else is already being paid to do that, but I also see where you're coming from, because I'm, convention would have it, supposed to be protecting your interests."

God, how I hated dialectical cobblers.

"It's not about my work outright," I offered dryly. "I hardly have the tools to take cement off the walls, right? It's a plus that it will come right off as soon as the mess is made, you see what I mean? Those grog-heads took one of my shirts I was drying to clean up their sodding mess. Can you explain that one to me then? Five years I've had that shirt. Five years it's survived our washers!"

Jake winced at the suggestion. For as wide a gaping hollow of what he did not know about building mainte-nance could fill, it did not fully escape his horizon that we washed all manner of sin and filth in those washers, not least of all the mop heads that absorbed all the happy accidents of the day . . . When you're hard-up, you give serious credence to some strange notions, though less strange than what little alternatives are already afforded you.

"I'll get you a new shirt. Don't concern yourself about it. Medium will do?"

"You'd better make it a bloody large. I'll want to breathe for a change."

"Large, then."

"Hey, you want to know what else is bloody and large, Jake?"

The temptation to bring the conversation with Alpha Prime, as we called him, to a new town record was fierce, though rules directly forbade influencing the momentum of discourse by suggesting the recurring topic, in this case Custard's Little Bighorn and the Peristaltic Wave from Hell, as I had just done, damn my stupid slack-jaw. I suppose even I should have anticipated the limits of my own cunctation, especially with six o'clock fast approaching from nowhere the blue and my services being sorely needed.

For you see, you could only palm off your work for so long before it acquired a – let's call it – undesirable quality. You must be able to make out the rough distinctions of your own face in the waters of your bucket as a rule, if you are wanting to escape a charge of dereliction; that is where you must draw the line, and not at all, I think it right to add, for fear it reflect the darkness of your own blighted soul.

"Is there anything else?"

"No . . . that'll be all, Wing Commander."

In the Accounting Department, I found Adrienne and Martine gabbing away about what I presumed had absolutely nothing to do with the numbers. I knew their racket well enough, having taken my liberties thumbing through the boxes they would have me trudge down to storage when the fancy overtook them. They were so full of deferred work that you could not deny that we were all the natural inheritors of a very distinguished tradition tracing all the way back from George Puttenham and right on to Huck Finn; but you have to tip your hat to someone else's brilliance when it finds you, and the system Accounting had set up for themselves was not something I could faithfully reproduce in my job description: I couldn't stomach, and nor was it right feasible, to tip buckets of bilge water all over the floor, only to mop it right up so people would see that your livelihood was all but justified.

Adrienne grew accustomed to the distinct sounds of my chewing – I had pulled out an eggplant that I'd brought for lunch and taken along for the ride sidesaddle of my flathead and Robertson – now that her office was temporarily housed in the anteroom where the lobby of the shelter had once been, its small rotunda amplifying sounds irregularly but to some discerning effect. I gave an inconsistent patter about my legs to try and throw her off; maybe she wouldn't recognize the sounds of sloshing food against my gums and might think that one of my legs was slightly shorter than the other, chalking one up to crooked chromosomes. She continued with her perfected strain of stuff with Martine, as I contemplated these laggards at play.

"Hoi, you!" I called, tossing a memento from our supply

shelves. "Something for when you're up on blocks."

"I should have known you'd run exactly at the moment we needed you most. Thank God for Terrence, or is it too soon to count our blessings?"

"Forget about that. You better watch what you say in front of staff when I'm around. They can't see for looking most of the time, but when you point them in my direction, you're not exactly doing me any favours."

"You sad sack. How mortified do you expect us to be if we get wise to your bone-idling? 'Caretaker in Flight: A Study in Inutility.' We all know what you get up to on your own – you've got it written all over your face."

"Alpha Prime is going to get on your case too if you're not careful about those spreadsheets, you dirty bean-flicker. You'd best mind your own grotty self."

"Alpha Prime?"

"Multivariate Marketing Analysis."

"Oh. The mouthful," Adrienne, catching on to my drift, responded. "Holly Blowlightly."

"It's no small wonder no one knows what he does around here with a title like that – he ain't figured it out himself. Don't think because of the new office he won't come poking around you hags."

"What the hell are you talking about?" Adrienne here gave a start, having not heard the latest. "Since when?"

"Effective this morning, he has absorbed your department into his. For good behaviour. He is a Master Adept in the art of Unrocking the Boat."

Martine at this time had scampered back behind her desk and began typing loudly. This should have been an indication of early onset for me: not failing to hear her typing, but for not tumbling its portentous significance – the Gloom of Doom himself, the Hour of Our Untimely Crossing, had returned.

"He's going to bleed you out, Adrienne, slow and methodic . . ."

"Just who I've been meaning to see." Alpha Prime's slippery rendition crawled up the back of my neck and died there.

"Hello again, Jake," I said, composing myself as best possible. "Which itch needs scratching this time?"

"Excuse me? No, I just wanted to talk to you about a few things."

"All right then."

Jake took out a fresh apple, an object with which he was unfailingly accompanied at all hours of the day, and rubbed it against his shirt where his kidneys were supposed to be: I was not completely convinced that he was not of a secret race of Moloch people sent to transmogorify our surroundings into the arid wasteland befitting the likes of the Loveland Lizard and Thulsa Doom.

"Well, first thing's your performance review," Jake said between munching mouthfuls of fruit. "It's just been brought to my attention that we need to have a powwow because it's been drafted for a few weeks now. You need to acknowledge you've received it."

"I'm busy with that emergency on the first floor women's right now, if you can't exactly tell, but when I'm free, I can let you know." Let's see how you handle that, you etherealized pockmark.

"Okay, that's great, that's really great. But we have to get these rolled out by tomorrow afternoon so . . . So today is going to be much better for everyone involved, I think."

"Well, I can't make any promises, Jake. The building has to come first, and it's almost suppertime for those swarming bints."

"Right, well, if you're not doing anything now, maybe you can step into my office for a light conference?"

Everything a question for this overthinking bastard. And for his every wrong turn, there would be Dr. No.

"I'm never not doing anything," I corrected. "You're busy or you're not, and as it happens, the women's lavatory requires my immediate attention, because Terrence has decided that he can't go in there after all. Adrienne was just telling me about it, which is why I'm here."

Jake turned to Adrienne, who at present was having a difficult time deciding whether to hang me out to dry or corroborate my story. It being not very likely that kicking away my ladder would mean a stay of execution for her departmental lapses, we could both see that she was in a better position, vocationally speaking, with me on her side than against it. The only question that remained was how convincingly above the mark she'd be. Give me my bloody point spread, you Tuckahoe hayseed.

"Right, it's a big mess, Jake," Adrienne said with a croak in her voice. "Seven kinds of horrible. I won't astound you with the details just this minute, but it's certainly something that will go down in the history books of St. Albans."

Kicked to touch you photo-finishing slag.

As I drifted away into the corridor, Jake called, "Before you go . . ."

"Yes?"

"I forgot to give you this memo. It's about the rash of complaints that have been coming in. We'll need everyone's cooperation on this. No ifs, ands, or buts."

"I'll have a look at it."

And so, though not without some considerable expenditure of effort, I was off, free from the glare of the scythe. If I'd had any ganglords to please, they would be slapping my back congratulating me at this very moment.

I trekked up the stairs to the second floor to show my face, before heading back down to make an appearance at the WC. I also wanted to give Terrence enough time to really get his hands in it, so that he wouldn't suddenly decide to tag me in halfway through on the job or worse, pull a Sunset Flip. If you think something putrid would put us off hanging around in the WC to count down the clocks, you can think again, as I'm sure Terrence was doing right at that moment. There was a control room next to the toilet stalls that you could easily slip in that led to the water heater for the showers and the pressure gauge, where you could easily while away a few hours with a ripping Plastic Man 80-page giant or a good book on Neoplatonic philosophy. Nobody minded you when you were in there, and you could always excuse yourself if you passed people on the way out because you had to check the gauge. You just turned your radio down nice and quiet.

I made for the men's lav instead, making sure not to be importuned by anyone along the way. Once there, and continuing along the mystery train of thinking over the hundreds of books I'd read inside, I pulled Jake's memo from my hind pocket. Unfurled in all its rearward glory, it took on a depraved kind of meaning.

To: St. Albans Staff
Subject: Information

So we are going to be responding to the tide of discontent and the ensuing drift of our clients to the "competition." Specifically Sally Ann and Seaton.

I need your help in compiling the necessary information in order to make our changes.

Specifically find out:
Do they have double beds?
Do they have mixed activity rooms? How many?
Do they provide breakfast?
Do they provide lunch? What specifically?
How far out can they schedule beds? A day? 1 week? More than a month?
How long before your bed is turned away? What time specifically?
Who are their main benefactors? Governmental or agency support? Specify what level of government.

I sense that it is the non-permanent social workers who are driving this discontent, so I think they are the best people to approach. But talk to anyone you have a relationship with.

We are on a mission.

Write down your information immediately and as accurately as possible.

— Director of Multivariate Marketing Analysis & Accounting

I could not decide whether to beat my head against a wall or flop on the floor like a mudskipper and die from laughter. It was no Sous Futura but it should do. Because when a dog is drowning, everyone offers him water. The first question drumming inside my head was whether or not this really was a memo being circulated to St. Albans staff, to Maintenance staff specifically, or if Alpha Prime had meant it for one pair of peepers alone and had intended to ensure such a result by hounding me all the merry long way to Accounting. I cleared the steps four at a time to the sub-level before smashing through the last landing and through the doors. I whipped out my keys, knocked the Shop door nearly off its hinges, and slapped the memo on the table. Terrence was there washing the sickness off his fingers and whiskers and as I expected, he barely acknowledged me.

"Olly olly oxen free!" I chirruped. "What's the score?"

"I know what you pulled, you bimbo. They all said you took one look in there and turned tail like your ex-husband was moaning for you."

I gave a smirk that threatened to make new sockets for my eyes.

"Hey sonny! I asked you for help the other day with transporting the chemical supply order and you left me holding the bag. On your bike, Wing Commander."

"Well, I'll take carrying a couple of boxes any day of the week over what I just did."

"Here, look at this. Tell me what you makes of it."

I studied the memo again intently over Terrence's shoulder. It was allegedly the first he'd seen of it.

"Where did you get this?" he asked, his tone suddenly losing its piquancy.

"You've never seen it?"

"Who gave you this?"

"Alpha Prime. He come 'round knocking."

"He's off his nut. You can't open your yap to perfect strangers about this kind of stuff."

"So you never got one of these? You're absolutely certain?"

"Yes, I'm sure. It's new."

I sank back in my chair and considered my narrowing scheme of options.

"Look," Terrence said kindly, the timing of which moved me to forget his plaguy insinuations. "I didn't say anything about your situation. We get enough stick here as it is."

I couldn't bring myself to offer rebuttals for once. Either Jake knew far more than he let on or I was just being overly paranoid, which for once rendered me without very many options.

"You don't have nothing to worry about," Terrence continued. "It's not like you're spare parts around here. If anyone's going to go, it's going to be van Leeuwen. Jeffries maybe."

I considered this advice closely. Jeffries was so unreliable that he could never be counted on to deviate from the letter of the law which his tasks were originally composed and assigned. Van Leeuwen, on the other hand, was also practically ready to retire from the human race, and went so far as to disconnect thermostats in the building so that he could tell staff that he could not change the set-points, saving him hundreds of useless pages. Maybe Terrence was talking sense, but I could still feel Jake's scythe whooshing about my head, circling for repeat manoeuvres. It felt as if all the piffling actions of the past lustrum were finally amounting to some lodestone heap of trouble. You started to grow defensive after thoughts like this: it was worth conning those hours for this long if I got sacked; even if he cornered me, I'd spin the room in my favour and he wouldn't have a prayer left in high heaven. Now was the time to drag the knowledge of every dirty secret and every dirty kickbacker in your possession out into the open and along with them a few hopeless bystanders.

"The funny thing is," I managed to say with only a mild dose of squeamishness. "I'm probably the most qualified person to answer his stupid questions. That's what I'm thinking about. Does that skunk know the truth about me?"

"You'll be the most qualified person *out of a job* then," Terrence said. "They're not going to stand for what you do here after hours."

I could do nothing but silently agree.

10.

St. Albans Homeless Shelter, Moss Park, Toronto, Canada, 1979

I FIRST GOT THE IDEA to live in the four penny coffins of our age in my third year at St. Albans. It's a wonder I didn't think of it sooner, what with the restless ratiocination of my useless lump – the final endowment gifted from my father, a brainbox spiralling out against rest. Leastways, it's not a big leap from wrestling rats to making peace with the idea of spending a few hours in a strange cot with another hundred restless souls hiccupping blood, sick, and dead nerves through the night. In order to have my Friday nights, I would sometimes not come into work at all, and make up for the lost work on weekends when the shelter was closed, all for the sake of a good bender. One weekend, just after I had fled Marjorie's place (I suppose that would have put me in my mid-twenties) and had only just started at the shelter, I forgot altogether to make up for the lost time, and only recalled it late Sunday evening as I was setting my head down for the final time. I chucked on my trousers and bolted out the door for St. Albans as fast as my poor rubbery excuse for legs could carry me. Somewhere amid the bladdered haze of sleep, I managed to buff a zigzag pathway across two whole floors, faintly resembling my initials – even with the horrors, my subconscious still raved for acknowledgment. After I bodged the rest of my duties, I awoke sometime later to Terrence turning on the lights of the building, turned over as I was in one of the cots normally reserved for the deadheads that came through for their morning paces, cheek by jowl the other buggers who managed not to choke on their own vomitus through the night.

In return for his silence, I had to pinch-hit for Terrence for six whole months, the savvy prick. Once a week, one of us would usually not come in for our designated shift at all and the other would perform the labour required of two people. Because I'd been caught with my arse over tit, I was forced to work an unconscionable five-day week for half a year for that rat-bellied fink. In retrospect, I don't think Terrence had it in him to really have me thrown out, but one remembers past betrayals so easily that soon everyone shares in *her* guilt.

But this fateful night spent with scabrous stink-biologies, coupled with my six-month jail sentence, led to my permanent decampment from my costly apartment carrying what little possessions I had for the higher calling of the best money-making scheme short of knocking off a bank and getting shot up to ragged pieces in the process that I, with my limited capabilities, could think of. Plus, my grandmother on my father's side was apparently in and out of debtor's prisons all her life anyway, so no one can tell me that my squalor comes even close to her blue-tongued wretchedness . . . so there's that.

With virtually nothing but the skin off my back and a bag of clothes, I lived entirely inside of my St. Albans locker, my existence condensed to its mean essentials. If things got a little too hairy, and I thought someone might suspect my extracurricular activities, I would stay at one of the other shelters in the city for a few days until the heat died down, and then resumed my residency anew.

The first week at St. Albans went well enough, though there were many occasions when my heart fell out of its cavity and wished for the comforts of hearth and home. I would shower in a scum-stained, muck-hardened basin with a low-pressure hose, and lather my hair in an all-purpose chemical cleaner while my clothes spun in our washers with the mop heads I'd just used to disinfect faeces from the walls. I would often work in the skin I was born in while my clothes dried, or enjoy the solitude of the doctor's cool, sanitized medical table with my literary heroes Woozy Winks and Win Jenkins close at my side to gladden my spirits – the right approach to the bespoke nonsense I was tailored for. When my stomach pricked up with complaint, the commissary was only a few yards away, where more than just cooling slop awaited my fingers.

St. Albans routinely received donations from the city's finest culinary greats, hoping to improve their standing among themselves – outdoing each other's charity and all that tosh. Anyways, the larder was always well provided with meat and dairy, so well-stocked in fact that there really was no finer privilege of my new accommodations than a four-in-the-morning American breakfast of six Balkan yoghurts, a half-a-dozen sausages, and a hot brew of coffee. What began for me as an illegitimated experiment in fiscal responsibility, suddenly took on the ears of a providence. I took home every red cent that I made that the state didn't have a hand in, having now rarely to pay for food and lodgings. I needed no longer to slough off daytime insults from the "clients," because I could now exact my crippling revenge on their beds: if there's ever two things that shouldn't mix, it's someone who makes your bed and knows your bowel movements like the comings and goings of the sun and moon.

But maybe there were other reasons for Jake's memo. I'd had a few close shaves of the boot in my time, counting up past reprimands. Maybe things had in fact built to a proper peak. Heading off the whirligig languor of the people of the abyss on a daily basis can stultify you, but on the day that a rat-faced gorgon and her washtub bustle lost her balance stepwise, carrying her newborn whelp no less, it was a lucky thing I'd been somewhat mesmerized by the God-defying proportions of her undercarriage. That baby would have been a broken bag of giblets had I not sacrificed a wonderfully prepared guava bannock sandwich to the stars above, all so that I could lean down on bended knee with arms outstretched like supplicating the Holy Mother (no guavas were hurt in the making of this story). But there was no word of thanks and gratitude, no commendations for saving that airborne child's life; instead, a charge of dereliction, as the stairs, technically falling under my purview of floor care, had not been properly relieved of their dressings. But you could no more tangle your feet around coils of dust and shreds of paper than you could on cushions of air. If you were lame and afflicted with bowlegs or raced up the flights with one hand over your eyes, you could certainly kiss the pavements because of those magic afflictions, but to no other causes attributed.

The rum bunch upstairs didn't see it that way, and I was summarily racked on the knuckles for it. Then, of course, there was the time, a few years before I'd made St. Albans my home, that I'd accidentally left one of the windows open in the kitchen because the smell of rancid meat had begun to infiltrate the higher offices. While Alpha Prime and his staff enjoyed the flavours of the high winds and the assurances of superior air circulation, the next morning it was an entirely different tune being sung. A kit of pigeons had decided that they were not above leaving their nests for a banquet of dried pasta and spent meat, along with the warmest toilet they'd ever set their mottled feathers on. Still, to be able to put the fear of pestilence into the beastly fowl swinging a broom in the air and finding a freshly laid egg in the kitchen sink is a sight I'll likely take to my grave knowing that days like that are infinitely more interesting than the humdrumming toil of flitting through papers and protocols in an office.

The mind will often purr itself awake when you have enough rope and is likely all you have keeping you from running into a wall reaching for the Living End and the keys of the kingdom. Naturally, I am reminded of the suicide protocols enforced at St. Albans: *Each Responder will be assigned a month in which they will be expected to respond to incidents wherein clinicians and counsellors need assistance. Methodology: The clinician will notify their team leaders of the need for the Responder. The designated Responder will then complete a ten question Self-Harm Risk Screening Matrix . . .* and so on and so on until your bollocks drop. It was like something out of the United Nations handbook.

Undoubtedly, this most recent transgression might have broken me in two – and then where would I be? All the beggarless years on the fiddle, safe from the streets and the knuckleheaded policemen, were beginning to catch up with me. When you've been dipping batteries in staff coffeepots for as long as I have, seen all the gippy stomachs and bawling outs from bureaucrats who, out of desperation of being rendered terminally inadequate, will make you their private sock puppet, you recognize a good thing when you see it, even if it comes down on you with the weight of a collapsing elephant.

I was soon brought back to my senses – is this where Serge went when he disappeared into himself mid-conversation? – half-realizing that I'd left Terrence and the Shop, and was making my way to Alpha Prime's office. I saw my own twisted monkey grip on my wrench, but soon recalling my-self, I replaced it onto my tool belt and wiped the sweat from my forehead. I dammed up all the violent impulses coursing through my body and wished for the strength to suppress them for a few hours longer. I looked out the windows of one of the activity rooms, hoping to catch a glimpse of receding sunlight to carry me away on the wings of some last-call optimism, but before I could get closer, I heard the holy Christian gurgle of a child's plangent wail-ing. Cracking open the window, and sticking my head out, I saw from six floors up a mangle of arms and heaving, flush faces; it was a drubbing out like no other, which resembled, from my elevated position, a crushed spider being stomped and slowly stirring back to life. A woman I saw only from behind stood not more than a foot taller than the girl who must have been hers; the presumed-mother used her size to her advantage, pushing down against her daughter's arms held up in an attitude of helpless defence. Then came the punishing blows to the face, and the child fell away to the floor again, but not before her frowzy assailant held her leg out for one more volley to the stomach. The child's cries grew louder, before diminishing into whimpers, and I stormed through a rumble of doors to the nearest stairwell, skipping steps two, three at a time (only a memo poten-tially ending your livelihood warrants four).

I screamed down the stairwell like a messiah on fire to ensure there would be no obstacles, and luckily enough found myself safely at the first-level exit door. My back to the inner wall, hunched over and looking out the corner of the wire glass, I saw the two cross the window, making their way to the front entrance. As quietly as I could, I propped the door open with a runner so I could get back inside if I had to, and approached the two at a distance of a few yards. They seemed to pay no attention to me. I picked up my squawker, and when they turned the corner, I paged Terrence, who was much larger than I was, to meet me in the front lobby, in the event the two of us would need to restrain the mother and escort her off premises.

"Mother Fistful is on a rampage!" I yammered into the box.

The woman gave her child one last chiding before entering the lobby to sign the register. I signalled the receptionist behind the desk in a series of inarticulate hand movements to keep them occupied and looked down the corridor to see Terrence running down and then slowing his movements as he neared us. When I turned to look at what the woman was doing with her daughter, my eyes widened with recognition and I could have sworn that her chattering teeth were giving off the distinct sound of typewriter keys. I stopped the circuitry of shock from flowing further through my body, because of the many eyes watching us. And even though I hadn't seen or heard from her in yonks, I knew it was *her*. She had aged (hadn't we all?), but she was unmistakable.

Terrence entered the foyer and I instructed him to follow me behind the main desk where Hanna, the receptionist, was seated.

"You missed one hell of a show," I said. "Well, I guess that's that."

"What the hell are you talking about?" Terrence hammered. "You should be filling out an incident report. You should know better."

"They'll forget about it soon enough. Don't worry about it I said."

"The police have been called."

"What the hell did you have to do a stupid thing like that for? I'm not getting involved with that circus ring from hell. Forget it. You talk to them if you want to."

"What do you want me to say, idiot? That I saw it through a brick wall?"

"I didn't call the police, you minger. I'm leaving."

And then he took the decision out of my hands.

"Call Jake and Adrienne, Hanna. They're the Responders for the week." Terrence glared at me with disappointment in his eyes.

When Jake arrived, he proved even more useless than usual. His clipboard was clasped against his chest like somebody ashamed of how they looked in a bathing suit, and his eyes scrambled for a place to rest on as I started explaining to Adrienne what had transpired. He stood dwarfed between the five of us assembled, including Hanna, unaware of the convoluted incident protocol he'd himself drafted ages ago.

Cherelle meanwhile sat on a chair simpering, eyeing me from top to bottom. I refused to make eye contact with her. I asked myself whether she was there with intent or by coincidence.

"Get sa faiseur la ene coup. Si li pas vantard li voleur," Cherelle said snidely.

Terrence turned to face her. "Eh?"

"Ignore it, she's, uh, probably damning you in some devil language."

"Is this about the women's?" Jake queried.

I elbowed Terrence hard into his side, turning my palm out at his front pocket.

"You haven't won anything," Terrence muttered under his breath.

"No one's taken care of the problem in the women's lavatory," Adrienne interjected. "It's been hours and everyone's been avoiding it. It's absolutely farcical."

"It's not about that," Terrence said, keeping his attention on the matter at hand. "If you'd just look to Mommie Dearest."

Finally seeing an opening primed for his area of expertise, Jake perked up and said, "Oh, I loved her in *Daisy Kenyon*."

The police came and went, escorting Cherelle and her daughter off-site. She didn't say anything to me again and I didn't try to reach her afterwards. She didn't come 'round again either, so I tried to put her out of my mind. Child Services made their visits, and after telling my story three hundred times over the telephone to everybody's sister, a detective said he wanted to meet me in person to corroborate the information I had given one final time. At last, the wits would be matched. My very own nemesis.

His swirling vacuum of questioning made me consider if I'd ever seen anyone so thorough in their applied execution of inanity, which coming from my mouth I realize is saying something. I wondered if perhaps he'd been coached in a new technique to get what they wanted out of us; a blessedly stupid and familiar approach of interrogation, with stratagems designed to snare guttersnipes into incrimination maybe, though it did not necessarily work on the higher class of guttersnipe to which I felt duly connected.

This dick they had come 'round to see me, plainclothes officer Holmes he said his name was, was crafty enough to lead me into the shadowy corridors of his cunning. To see if I could keep up, maybe. He reminded me very much of someone I was trying to eradicate from memory, even while I kept his codex in my locker at all times. How could I repay him that way, when he had attempted to fill in the gaps of my knowledge of the Sous during a time when he thought it mattered most to me? Holmes wasn't like the other constables I'd been talking to. For one thing, he didn't strike me as someone who came up very far from the people he was investigating; an inside track sort of feeling nudged up against me. The other sort were more liable to treat you like a criminal because of what spices your clothes smelled of, but me and Officer Bracegirdle here were cut from the same cloth – strategy or not, his method was so disarming as to make me prone to speaking plainly about things.

And so he talked to me as if we were old mates, and then occasionally perked up with a question intended to catch me off balance, or in a lie all knotted up. The first choice plum he plucked almost from the air was, "I just want you to know that there's no pressure here on you at all except to tell the truth about what you saw, as accurately as you can. Your testimony, however, will decide for us and Child Services what the future regarding the child will be." What a pot-bellied laugh you are good for, chief. What a nice lawn ornament you would make.

Question: Do you remember what happened?
Answer: I've been giving my version enough times to make me remember for a lifetime.
Question: Tell me again so that I can be sure.
Answer: Two pops to the face, one in the gut. No contest.
Question: Are you sure? You should know, some communities – they have different ways of handling things. The way they mete out discipline, for example.
Answer: This was no pitty-pat, if that's what you're asking.
Question: Is there any chance the mother was reacting in self-defence? That she was just putting her hands up and the child ran into her?
Answer: Hey mister, when was the last time, pushed or otherwise, you opened wide for a bolo punch?
Question: Are you some kind of nihilist?

Around and around we went, going over what I saw while he played noughts and crosses on his little pad of paper. I had filled my share of St. Albans incident reports beforehand, passed them on to Recourses, and Management had called me over and over again. Still I was expected at meetings about what had happened. This was going to be the end of all this horse-and-buggy noise in my head one way or another, and all I could think about was if I could only get Jake on this circular bent, my wallet would be a hundred dollars heavier tenfold.

"Look, the bottom line is," I said to Holmes, "I don't want to be responsible for this brat getting lost in the system. There's no telling she'll be looked after with a proper family, right?"

"That's right. They're not homeless, these two, but they come into the shelter to avail themselves of its resources, it looks like. But if we step in, there's a good chance the child will be removed. Is there any chance that the kick wasn't a kick?" It didn't exactly sound like a question.

"When is a kick not a kick? Said the actress to the bishop."

"Look, we can say on record that the mother just put her leg up to protect herself. Do you want to say that?"

"Why? If we did that, what would happen?"

"Well, we would keep a record that a situation like this transpired in the event that the information becomes useful, but ultimately the child would stay with her mother."

"How isn't it useful now? I'm understanding that the needs of the real world don't neatly conform to the way the law lays everything out, but my friend, I know what I saw. I'm not stupid." The gablou didn't believe you if you took the first way out – this would be true regardless of what side of the continent I was on.

"I wouldn't be implying anything different. I'm just saying that, given how you feel about not wanting to feel responsible for the child being carted off, this is maybe the most feasible, temporary situation that works best for all.

We'll say there were a few slaps on the face –"

"You've got to be joking me with your slaps."

"Yes, there was an altercation, which will be recorded, but the mother deemed herself fit to discipline the child in a suitable manner, so that the two could enter the shelter and proceed with – what time was this again? Dinner? This way we can avoid unnecessary heartache for all involved."

"Frankly, you can do whatever makes you happy. I don't know how many more times I can tell you a story before you get it the way you want it to sound." I was laying it on a bit thick, but you can't argue with results.

Link boys of Old London, sometimes a quick resumption of things is all you can ask for when you've been all but shot out of a cannon approaching terminal velocity. Cherelle was off the hook, the Sous were protected with their anonymity, and my St. Albans superiors were pleased as purebreds that I notified the Responders. Even more so to my credit, they were chuffed with my "commendable receptivity to discuss the matter in such explorative detail with the police."

Jake called me into his office a week after my last statement to the police, and ushered me into a seat that was a go-between of a New Age tuffet and a ratty banquette. It effectively placed you a foot lower than the surface of his desk and a few more below his gaze. By this time, I had eased myself into the thinking that my performance review was never going to come, though a small part of me knew that if there's one thing that civil service rejects are good at, it's the unshakeable belief that no task, however trivial, must go without sanctification, if only to confirm in their empty skulls that life, somewhere for them, holds meaning of a kind.

"This is a long time coming," Jake said, beginning a venerated line of pleasantries.

"I'm not going anywhere."

"That's exactly what I think is up for discussion. Tell me, how are you doing these days, health-wise?"

"Not that it's any of your business, but you'll be hard pressed to find a fitter specimen. For this work, I mean."

"It's come to my attention that we can do better in terms of the quality of cleanliness in the shelter."

"The results of your memo?"

"There's that, but we've been noticing a steady drop in the east wing being maintained at the level that we're comfortable with. The same goes for the commissary and the kitchen."

This was it. My belly lurched sideways as I awaited my sentencing. The active ingredients had done their work.

"Yes, it's not as if I haven't noticed either," I replied smugly. "You see things as you go by on your rounds, but your hands are tied all the same with daily responsibilities."

"We appreciate that, very much so. But we are being forced to consider certain alternatives."

"Oh?"

"It's not overly complicated. A significant portion of our funding is dependent on the level of impact we make on the community. These involve questions of visibility, brand language. You are aware of our competitors in the city?"

"Competitors? What do you mean?"

"The other shelters. If they can do more under the same funding scheme and provisions – God help us, if they do more with less – then it puts St. Albans in a very poor way. Accreditation is coming up in a few months and we can't afford to have the shelter looking in shambles."

"I follow then. What do you propose?"

"One option is to bring in a new janitor."

I could see the light, that awful, blinding, burning light. "Go to the light!" I heard myself think. Strangle him and then abandon yourself to the light.

"Well, I guess that's that," I said resignedly, letting my arms fall at my sides.

"But we have another idea in mind, one that is perhaps less time-consuming. How would you feel about working extra shifts? Say on weekends or a double when we would need you?"

"*Paid?*"

"Naturally, yes. We understand you're doing so much for the shelter already, and having seniority, we're obliged to circulate new positions internally first. Not so much a new position in your case, but you're our most senior staff member after Terrence. So . . . It's either that or we create a new relief position."

Away from the light, away! Fly back to this edge of darkness, where the frosted tangle of your men-at-arms awaits the second coming.

"That is . . . acceptable to me."

"Excellent. We'll draw up the paperwork immediately. There'll have to be an interview, but confidentially, I think I can tell you that you're our man. I mean woman. Congratulations are in very fine order."

I stood up as best as I could, picking up my feet with my hands because they had fallen asleep from discomfort. I turned for the door, but as I moved past his view, Jake called out to me and, from the sound of crinkling cling wrap peeling away, I could tell produced another apple for his delectation.

"I would also appreciate, when you have the time, information on any other shelters you have been frequenting for the past few years to supplement the information we have already collected. Perhaps I could press upon you as well to go so far as to recommend to your fellow patrons the amenability of our establishment."

The hairsplitting fuss-bucket had known the entire time I'd been diddling the company! Mo pas ouler croire! Though out of what exactly I doubt even he could peg with precision, considering the other patrons slept and ate for free. It was doubtful that my "promotion" came about because Jake recognized the "good intentions" that lay claim over my breast; more likely that there were easier questions to answer as to why an employee with a brass neck was getting all of a sudden more hours than why said floor-scrubber was suddenly out on her ear after she'd single-handedly avoided for the shelter some awesomely bad publicity or glory forbid, a violation of "brand language."

Thus, did my flyblown story live to see another day.

Before you could say, "I was born in an evil hour!" I was back to watching the breadcrumbs move from one end of the table to the next. I nearly quadrupled the amount of time I was skimming off the top on account of the fact that there was no staff to watch you on Saturdays or in the evenings, aside from the odd straggler who just couldn't keep away; and yet I still felt as if Jake had something over me, and would continue holding something over me until he dropped dead of ugly. There are no sure things in this life, and so you are left to sort out your business as best you can, with no hope for clemency. In knowing this, I began to consider how to square things between us in the most scandalous of ways.

Earlier on in life, I would have been prudent and not risked anything that would jeopardize the golden goose I'd been golden ticketed, but prudence was for the birds; I realized where my father came from, mentally speaking, and understood why he threw caution to the wind regularly and couldn't keep a job. I suppose the only difference between us is that I had thicker skin and could turn the other cheek. The Derwish would have arranged it so that someone like Darlo would have broken a geezer like Jake's fingers or had him hit by a car in the dead of night, but I didn't have the stomach for that like I had once believed. A man is no knapsack. So I couldn't be obvious now about how I got even with Jake, and neither did I want the off chance of being reprimanded again to endanger what fortuity had so reverently bestowed before me.

Inspiration kept itself firmly out of reach and I was left with the spent machinery of my tired brain. Luckily for me, maintaining the individual offices, which included keeping desks, cabinets, and drawers free of fingerprints, oil, and dust, came to be included in my extra duties, and I began to really get inside the old man's head – his habits and customs. In fact, you can make shockingly clear assessments of people based on the intimacies of their work environments, and grave pronouncements on questions of hygiene, attitude, and even political striping. Jake, as a helping hand of examples would testify, believed in hard and fast divisions, if the fastidious arrangement of his desk revealed anything. But at the same time, Management was there to manage and could not be troubled with other piddling considerations, and consequently, the rest of his office was an absolute sty, filled with discarded candy wrappers, bogies, petrified detritus from dead plants, and pair after pair of sweaty socks stuffed into his dress shoes. Such harsh contrapuntal arrangements did not suggest a mental break; it was far more pedestrian in nature, like so many others I tended to: he was simply being devoured inch by inch by his own hypocrisy.

The first germ of my revenge, however, grew from my discovery of a half-eaten apple inside his desk drawer, surrounded by the debris of excelsior, dust bunnies, and twines of his hair that had gone their separate ways and mutinied from his scalp. Days and days passed and still the obvious eluded me. It was only when I was changing a bin-liner one day, when I saw a decomposing apple core at the top of the heap, radiant and glistening like the aureole of the saintly angels, that epiphany beckoned loudly.

On a weekday when there was no apple to be found in

Jake's desk, I scrounged a representative candidate, subjected its merits to the scrutiny of my colleagues – some of whom volunteered to put it through its paces on the grounds that its captivations could be augmented – and found the time on the weekend to place it in a comfortable resting place. Sure enough, when I returned the next week to his office, all that was left in place of the apple that had seen what no apple should ever have been made to see, was an abandoned stem practically gurning to give me confirmation of my own twisted success.

11.

Sous Headquarters, Moss Park, Toronto, Canada, 1980

CHERELLE WAS WAITING inside her turquoise Allegro by the terminal entrance for arrivals. I loaded the car with Serge's substantial but surprisingly light trunk that I had dragged behind me, his only form of luggage. Serge and the *boy who said nothing* and I stepped inside quietly. Cherelle greeted my father felicitously. She was visiting her relatives a few cities over, and since she still felt guilty for grassing on me to her father about my whereabouts, along with a boatful of other indiscretions, she offered to pick my father up at the airport. I asked her to drop us off at St. Albans where, it being after hours (it was no longer an

all-night shelter), I made them all a hodgepodge of veg-
etables and chicken, and a bowl of middlings for dessert.
The three of them thanked me for my thoughtfulness, the
mute boy giving the most imperceptible of nods.

In the silence that followed our meal, I thought to myself how life had dulcified in my adult years in a way that
I hadn't considered thinkable as a child. There was much
misfortune in those early days, but the Sous could not have
it any other way. Sinon zot pu perdi zot charme, non? My
mother died at Stone House in 1974, pinballing around a
spiral staircase, a feat I imagine could not have gone un-
assisted; the Derwish similarly had his legs mown down
crossing the road on a red light, but was given satisfaction
when arrangements were made for the driver to be found
floating face down in the Thames by Teddington Lock. My
father in his turn was now finally returned to me after nine
years of fending for myself in Ontario; he surprised me
with the Souse's intention to settle here in Canada – communicated via an unmarked letter, care of the Derwish,
and then passed on to Cherelle – and to make good on a
promise he made me almost a decade before. I don't think
about whether or not he had been instructed by the Derwish or his hirelings to make contact with me, or if there
is another motive for his return. I accept that he is here.

Now that I could properly take stock of him, I saw what
ravages the years had worked over Serge. He had no hair
left – karro cane prends dife. His face was riddled with
lines that his eyes seemed ironically to welcome, and his
skin was blotchy and scabbed over with illness. It was like
looking at something chaffing with inactivity at the pawn-

brokers, waiting to be picked up by its owner. All this disrepair, even though it seemed he was now in clover, for all those years gone hard by. He was wearing an orange plaid, tailored suit and a neat straw boater on his head. The sight reduced me to tears, in spite of the opulence it conveyed. There was something disestablished about him all the way down to how he leaned on his weaker leg while standing, pitched his chin down when listening to questions. Our first embrace at the airport confused him something wicked and blighted, even more so than my circumspection over the mute teenager who he'd arrived with.

Enough time had passed that our ways of interacting were suitably altered. Distance, avoidance over the years, had cooled our nervy tetchiness. Like a glancing moment of clarity, we were happy to leave the logomachies to the past. We talked to each other like civilized people, or the most we could approximate it.

I passed across the table the codex Malbar had left me all those years ago and which I had concealed from my father until today. The mute boy seemed to look at it covetously, while Serge eyed it without breaking his concentration from the remainder of his meal. Before telling me he had no use for it, he said he was surprised I could cling so dramatically to the past. I told him that I kept it on behalf of him and Malbar, to remember where I came from, even if I wanted nothing to do with it. He advised me to perish it from my memory if I ever hoped to live down the opprobrious influence of the Sous. Cherelle meanwhile performed admirably the behaviour we had come to expect of her, looking around, unsure if she was wanted at all.

"What the hell is this place?" Serge asked me.

"St. Albans. Where dreams go to die," I said. "Then cheat death."

Sergent laughed, and I swear an entire floret of broccoli came sailing out his nostrils. Then he told me that he was tired, so I directed him to one of the empty cots, pointing my finger to the space behind a half wall.

"Is this temporary or will I be staying in this dungeon the entire time?"

"Temporary, but no expense spared."

"I need a favour, by the way. A few favours, actually."

"What?"

"I need you to hold on to my luggage for a few days."

"Langet tor ma," I cried in disbelief. "What the hell did you smuggle inside?"

"Malbar."

"What, you mean metaphorically?"

"No, not in the least."

The tattered trunk was wrapped in a dulled fustian cloth in which I imagined what assemblage of mouldering flesh and bones could rest within its confines. I was transported to the last time my eyes met with those pallid greens whose sockets threatened now to stare back blindly at me. The last of the day's light crept through the mullioned windows and limned my father in a salvific string of light, as if God was consecrating my father's actions with approbation. Serge went on to describe how year in and year out, when he went to pay his respects on the anniversary of Malbar's death, he'd find voleur-caveaus at the poorly tended tomb. The robbers were unearthing the casket to sift through Malbar's pockets and teeth for gold and silver, though they'd happily settle for any metal that could be melted down and sold for drink money. All they could find though were souvenirs of the Sous group my father had thought it expedient to bury with his comrade, only to later find the secrets of his childhood laid on display at the Port Louis bazaar for any French excursionist to see. These grave-robbing tatterdemalions would sell mourners flowers, only to remove them from the gravestones minutes later to be sold again to the next unlucky batch of soft-headed divs come their way. Impressed by their coordination and efficiency, my father offered them membership in the Sous. Serge now pointed to the boy he was travelling with, introducing us finally.

"We call him Piom."

"On approval?" I asked.

"He's a bright boy. Maybe a future ahead of him. He helped me get the body out without arousing too much attention. Then we ground Malbar to dust."

If this did not enkindle my heart to a sympathy with my father's intentions, then his dejected face tilting skywards, sucking back on his pottage using kangaroo care, certainly did me in.

"What's the other favour?" I asked impatiently.

"We need to hold another Sous meeting for the Ontario chapter. Big numbers, so bread and circuses, make a nice big show. This space should accommodate nicely."

"I'll not be here then. You can use the space between midnight and six in the morning and I'll only be on hand to let you in and out."

"It's a good thing you agreed, otherwise I'd have you with eminent domain."

"You will not be seen, am I understood?"

"Not seen, but understood."

The following night, the shuffling, huddled Mauritian masses came grumbling through the back doors, out of the sopping wet of the rain no less. I read through portions of Malbar's codex for the first time as I manned the doors. I skipped to the end, dated the fall of 1970, four or five years after Malbar's death – my last night in Brixton, hence its confessional nature, but by whose hand? The notes told me that Serge would spend years roving from one place to the next at the behest of the Sous leaders, smuggling goods out of Mauritius to every corner of the globe that housed a Sous member, minister, whatever, wherever. He had been on the other side of this arrangement for the better part of twenty years, getting fat on smoked sausages, peanuts, guavas, biscuits manioc from the Rault Biscuiterie. No remedy but patience. This gruelling posting rotated on a yearly basis, usually the result of a hasty nomination and balloting process, but in typical fashion, my father had evaded this civic obligation longer than any other Sous member by wangling his way through the clutches of his overseers, pegging it on Malbar's shoulders for years. Until of course, he was slammed with a stiff penalty amounting to holding the post for the years he spent absent from my life. It didn't take a lot of thinking to guess which manzer-fes petitioned for the penalty in the first place. Owing to my present friendship with Cherelle, and the fact that the perpetrator could no longer walk, I figured Sergent had let bygones be bygones. *Pede poena claudo.*

I quietly folded the codex closed and placed it inside one of my pockets, when who should make an appearance? I held the door wide and placed a plank of wood over the three steps leading from the back lane so the Derwish could wheel himself through. He took my hand, pressed it hard without saying anything. The softened look in his eyes registered appreciation.

The commissary was chock-a-block with people I had never seen before, pustular with lowlifes and thugs. There were so many people that there weren't enough chairs to hold them all. A good half of them were pressed up against the walls and against each other, all vying for a view of the centre table, where my father, Pourri, and the Derwish were seated. Rag-and-bone men with pots slung over their shoulders puttered around in circles, bookies cleaned their noses and groomed themselves leisurely. The nanier a foutes who were barely bothered enough to attend were mithering about the raffish accommodations. Anyone who beat out Her Majesty's pleasure found their way into our scumhole to dish and dawdle, to drudge and dinge, and whatever else was in store for the night. Before the commencement of the proceedings, Pourri apologized for the Bowling Green's continued absence at meetings, citing his inability to make any connecting flight on time. Pourri assured the members that the Green would resume his duties at the beginning of the new month, that receipts for their dues would be tabulated as swiftly as humanly possible.

"Thank you for consenting to leave your homes on this

February filldyke morning," Pourri intoned. "We know it has not been easy for some of you, and your commitment to order has been noted. We are up to the thwarts with members tonight, and this should be taken as the advantageous gauge of our prosperity that it is."

I mimicked these words under my breath. An older man who was vaguely reminiscent of someone I could not place, and who stood beside me with a wry neck, took his notice away from Pourri. He elbowed me in my ribs. When he addressed me, he looked as if there was a dirty word written on his temple that he was trying vainly to read.

"That's a mighty good impersonation," he said. "But you should have more respect for these gentlemen. They've brought us up out of the dark ages! We have representation now."

I took my screwdriver out of my back holster and stirred his coffee for him.

"You look a little green around the gills, my son. Make sure you are getting enough iron."

I stepped away from the meeting, and clawed my way back to the cots that I had arranged for the night. Half of them had been disturbed by attendees who needed something to do and had no better alternative than to twirl their bottoms into my turned-down beds. Over echoing outpourings, I found myself a nook where I knew I would not be noticed. I pulled out the codex from my pocket once more. I leafed through its pages again, skimming through its illiterate protocols and half-scribbled vendettas with care this time. I realized then that its defining feature was that it was annotated in red ink by Malbar's hand. *Sous*

Codex #M04-1965. Diable p marier en bas pied piment. My life's intermittent phases. Chapter the first . . .

One portion of the book held my interest more so than any other. On the endpapers at the back of the book, which I had somehow missed moments earlier, Malbar had bled out the thoughts of his acceptance into the group. He rants about a police officer that won't relent in a gutless crusade to arrest children coming of age for petty infractions of the law, who invents bogus charges on which to incriminate even the most pathetic of ne'er-do-wells . . . *A devil of a liar. Nothing short of World Class Superlative. He looks like shit at a tea party though.*

This officer's mother is a proud, matronly poulterer who inherits a tannery from her father in the twilight of her life. She invests all her hopes in her son continuing either of her trades after she passes, clearing away the mystifications of chicken and leather preparation, and starting him on his way with a post as a lowly attendant in her Taylorist pantry. Instead, the son finds himself disposed to *more fraternal obsessions.*

The constabulary ensorcells him with the prospect of city-wide recognition – electrifying his senses. But he is able to disobey the orders of his mother only after completing a solid decade's worth of work at the tannery, a feat of endurance that will serve him well in later years, especially in his travels as a smuggler. *Sergent taking over for me because I have the sickness. Leave it to him to try to outclass a dead man. I leave as a corpse. What's his excuse for looking the way he does?*

The mention of my father gives me pause, as I recall the

discussions over Serge taking Malbar's place in the smuggling operations, worked out days, months in advance of the Blue Boar meeting.

The poulterer's son is forced to find able replacements so as not to shame the family business. Three childhood friends, but more importantly, former employees of the poulterer herself, whose collective intellect, capability, and application can successfully masquerade as his own person before the failing eyesight of his mother, are chosen. The Derwish handles the business operations, the Bowling Green the accounting, and Pourri provides the barrel-chested services of muscling out competing merchants. The poulterer's son leaves the family business in safe hands, while he *polices infested gutters and canals of Port Louis. Stuck with Deathrot, Liferot, and Crotchrot at helm. At least Serge was top bloke, easy to get along with.*

I have to check myself from thinking that Malbar has become confused in his last days and is crossing wires in the case of where history is concerned, that even a purposeful error handled with coordination is still an error. There is too much conviction in his voice to suggest something malapropos. It is the lies that I have been fed that are out of keeping with Malbar's confession.

The *poulter-son* begins to regret this decision when news spreads that the Mauritian Police Force are not planning on renewing their existing contracts with their equipment suppliers. The M.P.F. are looking at local leather alternatives to provide holsters, slings, and belts on a mass, nationwide scale. Grievously sensing a career mistake, the *poulter-officer* prostrates himself before his former colleagues, begging to be allowed back into the fold of business operations. *Sergent is making mess of pants right now because he's bet on the wrong horse. This is what professionals in our trade term "selling wet blue to a wholesale upholsterer" or stupid way to give away money.* Reluctant to split the already thrice divided profits into a smaller sum to accommodate the return of the young constable, the *Trinity of Idiots* grudgingly accepts him as a consultant, ignorant as they are of the finer points on sammying and fatliquoring. *These blockheads try to curtain coat a rawhide by urinating on it at intervals.* Before long, the tannery is responsible for most of the country's leather production, which is how the Sous hit upon the idea of the sale of illegal passports, based on their already extant contracts to provide the leather used in state-issued passport books. The only trouble is that authentic passports are only good for getting out of the country for a spell – never permanently. The Sous begin to stifle under the short-sightedness of this scheme. Itching from barely below the surface is the feeling that greater opportunities can be seized if only someone is vainglorious enough to stand and take notice of them, *but in Pourri's case it actually is just crotchrot.*

Leave it to Officer Sergent to "consult" his way to an equal share of the company to which he once bore sole ownership. He devises ways to exile his countryfolk on the allure and promise of the first world's convenience – through *a bellicose kind of hucksterism* no less – only to later help emigrants repine for the same country they feel ejected them in the first place through her lack of concern and unnerving economic minginess. This is achieved through postcards, delicacies past their sell-by date, or a musical strain or two of their native tongue; anything to remind wearied travellers of the ties that bind them hard and fast.

The four Sous, who outgrow the prepubertal charm of petty crime, only lack a way to lend their toings and froings between countries an air of redoubtable fatality. A *Réunnionais sot, or so they call me*, employed at the tannery as a scudder, and whose greatest philosophical achievement is in the proposition that he can no longer kill himself with impunity – *Ican'tevenbringmyselftobuytherope* – because he has given birth to a daughter (*noblesse oblige*), provides this assurance. The Sous had known the Réunnionais for years, but were mindful of his otherness. *They don't like the sound of my fricatives...* They returned his overtures of friendship with laughter for a time. *They hate me.* Until the day they discover that his unique, exploitable citizenship can give all future Sous migration an air of emigratory imperium. *They love me.* The Sous are reborn on that day, reborn into something more odious and worldly. My father, the discredited constable, secures this majestic future with the masterstroke of marriage. *Serge takes Virma off my hands. I am a free man again.* Then, he asks his friend and future father-in-law Malbar to sponsor him as a French citizen of Réunion Island.

After reading these revelations, I spat across the whirlpool of forlorn faces gesticulating in a frenzy. I felt unsettled. That was Serge's greatest lie if there ever was one. Perhaps an ex-career in policing was particularly valuable in smuggling operations. I didn't want to believe that Serge had been the policeman the entire time, but it made a knotty kind of sense. I was brought back to my brief interaction with Officer Holmes. There was something familiar about him, after all. How things could have worked out differently if Serge had stayed on the right side of the law when we emigrated. Why, a mere equivalency exam could have made Officer Holmes and Officer Mayacou practically bosom buddies. I spat again for good measure.

The Sous pilgrims were still hanging on intently to every word being discussed by the three grizzled drizzleds. I now noticed that the Derwish was wearing my *grandmother's* mantelet around his shoulders, only now it was decked out in white polka dots the size of apples, with passport stamps in the middle of them. He was holding forth at the centre of the dining hall like a character from a mystery play. Pourri was presently treating a melamine ladle as if it was the Holyrood, thrusting it in the air over and over again screaming, "Back, you spikenards! Back, I say!"

All these sad men and women in attendance had left Mauritius with the gleam of dreams in their eyes. Malbar's Réunnionais associates sponsored them as relatives, and then these emigrants found themselves stranded in foreign climes, penniless and unable to go back.

The Sous had deliberately picked for their candidates the most inept and dependent of undesirables, so that they could not help but congregate at the dead hand of Sousian gobbledygook, as they did today, and four more times each year. They paid exorbitant premiums just a few hundred dollars shy of a pair of plane tickets, so that they could have a small flavour of home, a memento from their loved ones, all the while brandishing their five-cent rupee coins on their lapels or buttonholes that have long since become their badges of identification between one another, lost in the alleys and roads they found themselves aimlessly wandering. These dejected souls abandoned all purpose and character, and perhaps even mistook being passed over in a crowd for the highest form of assimilation. Their language evolved, their grammar poked around, their phonetics bent and curved with the angularity of a drawl. Yet they survived on account of their awe of the happy land before them and their obeisance to its customs, because survival never asks for much more than an indignity or two for good measure. The fatliquor people had treated their charges as they would a side of rawhide, positioning their victims between opposing ends of desperation and hope.

And thus the heavens and the earth, the Mauritians in their wastelands and the house which my father built, since conjoined with mine own house of the wretched refuse of your teeming shore, were completed in all their vast array. So We blessed the last day and made it holy, because on it We rested from all Our work that We had done in creation.

"Ki kote twalet la?" an attendee asked me, taking notice of me lying down and reading.

"A droite."

Cherelle came from behind the faceless pilgrim to sit beside me. I passed the codex to her.

"I've seen it," she said plainly. "I read mine as a child."

"Good reading, I hope."

"I like the poulterer story. It's clever and all, in its way.

How everything in the codex is written in a way to mystify the police. They all know the head arrangement. All one sprawling flea-flicker written in crayon."

"Merde dimoune. My head hurts," I groaned, having been duped like I was a child again. "How do you mean?"

"I don't know what it says in yours, but don't believe even half of it. Especially the bloodlines. Can you really imagine my father mending roads like Pitkin? Oh God. Uncle Sylvan's no General Schreiber, no military man either. He doesn't make eye contact with his *barber*. Do you remember that meeting in the Blue Boar? Well, did the four of them look like brothers to you? 'Cause they can't all have had the poulterer as their mother . . ."

"Hmmm. I'm at a loss for words if I'm honest with you. Do any of these meetings get your motor running? Like the old days, I mean."

"No," Cherelle said. "Not for a long time now. I'm not even sure my dad has his heart into it. He's just going through the motions. Not sure about Pourri though. He's come on like gangbusters."

We looked at Pourri marching down an aisle between pilgrims with a riding crop clasped in his hand, except the leather tip had rupees glued to it. He looked like he'd gone to seed. He walked past men, thwacking anyone at the elbows that wasn't maintaining the orderliness of his line. "Golnar, from Golnar family! Cheong, from Cheong family!" the Derwish called out, as pilgrims advanced to their table, greedily awaiting which items they'd requested had bypassed the Canadian customs office. Most faces turned away from Serge and the Derwish in low spirits, though more often than not begrudgingly chewing on a foot-long smoked sausage cut in two as they walked away. The pilgrim who jabbed me was comparing his parcel from his family with what I guessed was an itemized list they had sent him through the mail, outside of traditional Sous postage routes. His envelope bore none of our postage stamps. Noticing this, I stood up to confront him, resting a hand on Cherelle's shoulder to stop up her talking in the politest way I knew how. I changed my mind and instead made my way to my father. Pourri blocked me from getting closer.

"Sorry, can't let you pass," he said oleaginously. "If it can wait, you have a better chance seeing him after we're done for the night. Between you and me, just for appearances' sake. Can't let these crumbs think we're picking favourites."

Pourri gently directed me to the back of the line. Again, another pilgrim asked me, "Ki kote twalet la?" and once more I directed him to the lavatory. In the corner of my eye, I saw the door slowly swing shut (its hinges needed to be oiled), and noticed a small multitude congregating inside, including No Stamps. This spelled big trouble, my bones were telling me. I expected that I would have to restock the entire lavatory, but instead I overheard on my approach animated and disillusioned squabbling.

"Ene la trappe sa. La police immigration pu vini coma dire mouche du alouda limonade!" a voice I thought belonged to No Stamps vociferated sourly.

Cherelle, inheriting my sense of alarm, also began to take notice of various pockets of individuals assembling outside of Pourri's line. Cherelle was presently behind fifteen or so pilgrims looking at the St. Albans awards cabinet. Imprecations erupted from the pilgrims' lips. Seeing me approach, Cherelle jogged towards me to keep me away.

"What are they looking at?"

"Your T.E.A.M. Award," Cherelle said. "The one commemorating your work with the police? What is that about?"

"Aio mama oh, ki lengrenage mo fine tomber . . . !"

By this time, my father had begun to take notice of the river parting of people in his field of vision. I looked at him, and then nodded my head upwards in the direction of the exit behind him. He handed off what looked like a bottle of wine to the woman in front of him, then signalled for Piom to come to his side. Piom fleered in Serge's direction, and walked towards the selfsame exit I was motioning to.

Suddenly, and with the same force I was accustomed to hearing it smash outwardly, the male lavatory door was kicked wide open. No Stamps brandished a ballcock, ball float still attached, in his right hand.

"Fouille partout de fond en comble," he rallied. "Checker ki zot fine coquin!"

So they were after what the Sous had stolen from them, which made a terrible amount of sense, I was sad to admit. The next little bit would not be easy to surmount. Not the off-chance of calamity, but sick-to-your-heart guarantees.

"They can breathe life into dead animals," another member of the crowd screamed. "Let's see them breathe life into themselves after we've done 'em in!"

Without more fanfare, all was pandemonium. Pourri

charged at No Stamps with both arms extended over his head, which he brought to bear over his opponent until he was No Face. A flood of forty or so people streamed out of the men's lav, which had as its tributaries the people by the awards cabinet and a few others by the Accounting office. Pourri was sent flat on his back by the onrush of people. A naked man stepped out of the lavatory carrying a toilet seat cover and the rest of the pilgrims made themselves scarce screaming, "Pillywick! Pillywick's here, get out the way!" A few who remained loyal to the Sous made a barricade of flesh around the head table. Cherelle was trying to wheel her father to an exit amid ceiling-fan-arcing bowls curving downwards, made more unbearable by the refuse from the bins assailing us. Then came the stale Yorkshire puddings.

I found Piom in an earthquake position beneath an exit door, unsure if he was meaning to block it or if he felt it the wisest place possible from some safety procedure he incorrectly associated with the situation at hand. Making easy work of him was merely a question of how hard to slash the air in front of me with a Torx. He shrank away, clawing at the jamb. I grabbed him by the scruff of his neck before I threw him out on his ear. He landed on some bags of rubbish, not seriously hurting himself, but the pressure his body exerted on the bags propelled a horde of maggots formerly contained within them into the air, whereupon they sprinkled down about his crown and shoulders, burning the air with a stercoraceous lining.

Some of the shelter regulars were milling about outside waiting to be let in, as opening hours were less than an hour away. I called a few by name to help me.

"Charlie! Rusty! Hey Freddie! I've got a sawbuck for each of you for twenty minutes of your time!"

The three men cut to the front of the line, looking past Piom as they went inside. I let them into the building quickly. The sounds of violent commotion continued from the dining hall. I could faintly see Pourri pushing someone into the ceiling fan, hoisting him up by his collar and belt loops.

"The man in the wheelchair, the woman protecting him, and the geezer in orange plaid," I instructed. "Get them outside safely. Don't louse it up!"

I galloped to Adrienne's office, going around the dining hall along Trade Route Five. I fumbled for my keys and managed to trip over no fewer than three chairs in the cramped office. I dragged my father's trunk case over my shoulder. As I was locking up, I could feel that I was being watched; this I could tell over their laboured breathing. No Face was covering the side of his head with a bleeding hand, while the other supported himself against the wall.

"Coma to capav faire sa avec to propre race?" No Face wheezed.

"Take it on the arches, No Face."

"Kete?"

I dragged the unconscious No Face and the trunk to the second floor, propped open a window, and slumped my freight out the opening. I followed behind, filing a mental note to shut the window before leaving should the carousing come to end before I was out of a job. I met Cherelle, the Derwish, Serge, and their saviours in the alleyway, without so much as a hair mussed from their heads. Rusty and Charlie were holding Piom fast between their arms, and he squirmed every now and then, looking like toothpaste someone was trying to wriggle back into the tube.

"Here's your other rabble-rouser," I said to the onlookers.

Serge was looking through the top of his straw boater, which had been peeled back like a can of Campbell's soup.

"About time," Serge said. "Bring him here."

"What do you think, Serge?" Derwish asked.

"I think he's a fuck sight better than we could hope for. Give him a few weeks to nurse off the beating he's taken before we put him to work again."

"What are you nattering on about?" Cherelle demanded.

"Don't throw a strop," the Derwish said. "You probably just don't remember him. You only met him once, when you were young. That's Darlo, the Menaceur – dans dilo, 'in over his head.'"

"Explain," I said bluntly.

"It's what the position entails. He's the patsy, the gudgeon, the heel. He's our man, on the inside, like. Pourri and him put on quite a devil of a show."

"They're a little advanced in years for this nonsense, don't you think?"

"You and Cherelle were to replace them. Before plans changed."

"What's all this then, your bread and circuses?" I looked to Serge for answers.

"This is good housekeeping, *fouineuse*, like your waiting area keeps reminding me," Serge stated. "We're having trouble carting off so much luggage through too many checkpoints. This lightens the load a sight, not to mention drives up the value of our services, due to scarcity. Those that re-up anyway. Market conditions are favourable."

"Tire kaka mettre pete."

"*Exactement.*"

"And Piom?"

"We'll see how he manages without a support group on this side of the world and without speaking a lick of English. Nothing without your newspaper translator, are you boy?"

"Is there any point in my going back to work in a few minutes?"

"Pourri already has the insurrectionists at gunpoint, toeing the line," the Derwish reassured. "They are helping restore order and the condition of the premises in which we were welcomed. Thank you for that."

"Coma to capav faire sa avec to propre race?" a disoriented No Face, née Darlo, repeated.

A welter of the sausage-witted, pulverized seditionists lay prostrate on the tiled floors. They were then gathered up and had their goods confiscated, banned from the Sous for three years. They would have to pay heavy amercements should they desire new applications, which of course all of them did. The cycle was such that the ousted members never outstripped the incoming "birth rates" of new members. This delicate balance in harmony was chief among the Green's responsibilities. Apparently his absence from such meetings ensured his unflagging impartiality managing admissions, even if no one had seen him in person for quite some time, maybe since the Kadadac Incident.

Yet wherefore the enduring survival of our derelict people? To what grace the raw power of these schemers? Where else but the many children, siblings, acquaintances, comrades willing to abet the happiness of their devoteds, kith and kin who comprised the enablers, sympathizers, and even enemies. All points of discourse intersecting into a lightning array of action and inertia. Like I myself did when Malbar's remains, distributed and contained within eleven cheddar cheese tins and wrapped in a pair of disintegrating pajamas, were conferred to me for safekeeping, given how I'd kept his codex free from harm and prying eyes for so many years and the nature of assistance I provided at the shelter (now the new Sous headquarters in the sleepless hours of the night). And though my acceptance into the group was delayed by my infractions – failing to follow my father's orders to find work outside of the Sous, and later and much more seriously, being unable to resist the wandering thoughts of a psilocybin-induced delirium, going so far as to put the codex on sale to the Roundman – it is decided.

I am trusted with the fifty other codices insulating Malbar's cheesy ashes from the many bumps in that trunk's diverse, happy travels. But the codices need reworking for a modern age, need updating and legibility for new threats on a Perspex-composite horizon, shimmering like a rainbow of new viability. The disaster with Piom has proved that much of the logic of greying temples needs to be not so much challenged, as improved upon.

"Aka Aka Boule Caca Les Veres Les Veres Mayoner Ister Ister TAC" – this one's off to Brighton, this one's off to Stroud, this one's running his dole rounds keenly, this one's sold his plow. That one can't be trusted, that one knows too well, that one's sold down the river, and drowns for quite a spell. That sort of thing, per Serge's communiqués. He beams with puddles of pride on the day that I hand him fifty new, hardbound codices the size of matchboxes, each containing some stolen or allegorized plot from *The Bulldog Breed*, *A Stitch in Time*, *One Good Turn*, *Up in the World*, and countless other Norman Wisdom films. He approves of the liberties I take, but mainly the orders I follow, and the new assignments I concoct for his peers to be delivered with their new documentation are well-nigh flawless.

I work best at obfuscations, have five years' worth of it in fact from my time at St. Albans – a skill bound to improve further with time. Pourri needs alibis for certain dates, which I scribe into a loose timetable that looks more like a mandala than a rap sheet. The Derwish insists that his relationship with the Green be explicitly maintained, much like my father's stories' interconnectedness with Malbar's, though I can't make some of the particulars stick. The Derwish even asks that I review the documents attributed to Cherelle, which I doubt she even knows exist. She is happy to be a chauffeur for the gang, and her father's keeper. I, on the other hand, marvel in fear at the possibility that the codices reveal too much of the truth of the Sous activities. Serge champions the demented wisdom of his policies regarding the truth to be infallible. They are insurance against infiltrators reading the codices and abandoning the feasibility of *all* information contained within, alibis and all. We are all givealittles then, mining and miming the heuristic world for a solid ounce of possibility, a vast metabolic network of propositions, equivoques, sufficient causes, and truth-functions. So began the world, so becomes the world.

My final task is to account for my own presence among the Sous, as a testament-taker and witness to their activities, their Grand Archiviste. This is my father's only gift to me, in a life known for its tyrannized privation. To bear witness, and to give account of my journals, through the privilege of a tourist, of the life of the small-time and its heathen impedimenta. Go forth, knowing thyself a sear imitation of a woman, daughter of a tarradiddling island rover, with the shame of things to come tailing behind her. There are other stories to recount, *bien sur*, of the nabobs bankrolling these enterprises of crumbling dust and island particulate, of Pillywick, the day tripping Sous commando assassin, the mescal button politicos in the Sous Court of Appeals, Malbar's last days, and his persecution by a recurring dream of rabid dogs chasing him without his trousers on, for fear upon his death that his minders neglected to bury him with his nightshirt on – all worthy, goodly tales of palm-shaded profligacy, but deserving only of mention, and never more than partial confirmation, outside of their own hardback tomes. All things *picayune* have now wandered their way under my compass, straight-sighted and true, accompanied by the manginess of the slums, the bowed spirit of a querent, and the quietude of a seer.

Glossary

Tukmaria: Basil seeds.

Alouda glace: Mauritian milkshake.

Sa gogotte la enne voleur . . . mange, divertir, caca: That dick is a thief. He never works. Where do you think he gets his money to dress like that? He's an asshole: he only knows how to steal, eat, gallivant, and shit.

Sousoute: Cunt.

Ti Pourri: Literally, "small-rotten."

Gablou: Police.

Avant ki mo tane rumeur la: Before I hear that rumour.

Li content sali nom . . . casse so la guelle: He likes to sully the names of people; that's why they broke his jaw.

Montagnes pas zoine – dimoune zoine: Mountains don't meet. People meet.

Eskiz mwa: Excuse me.

Mo pa pou repeter: I won't repeat myself.

To tousse mo ti fi encore . . . pilon: If you touch my daughter again, I'll break your back, you faggot.

Erezman toulmonde conne to fatigan: Luckily everyone knows you're tiresome.

Trwazyem fois mon dire . . . sulazman ici: That's the third time I've said to leave the children at home. There's no relief here.

Pe nas trakase: Don't worry yourself.

Kok depaille: Hairless cock.

Les guels kok: Penis-face.

Pinere: Cheater.

Plok Poners: Idiots.

Mo pou zigeler toi: I'm going to fuck you.

Gogote: Dick.

Souslard avant sous terre: "A drunkard before underground." Alternately, "a drunkard before I'm dead." The pun of the word "sous" is lost in the translation.

To faim: You hungry?

Cot to billet: Where's your ticket?

Kadadac Bar: Kadadac is the onomatopoeic sound of a child piggybacking and bouncing on someone, possibly referring to the hooves of a horse trot.

To pu mange tous sa la: You're going to eat all that?

Hmmph . . . dans Canada: Hmmph. You don't learn French here in Canada?

Boule caca . . . roule caca: "Ball of shit," and "roll shit together" (as one would a snowball), respectively.

Dire moi ene coup (ki qualite couillion sa): Tell me something (what kind of idiot is this?).

Ti zom: Small man.

Rotin Bazar: A switch, primarily used for beating.

Chamarel: Mauritian city, but also a game of hopscotch.

Capave croire mo codex: Can you believe my codex?

Mo pou alle gris gris: "I'm going to Gris Gris" (a Mauritian city), but also a play on "mo poil gris gris," meaning "my grey pubes."

Pistache pourri: Rotten peanuts.

Sintok: Pejorative for "old Chinese person."

Ti pete: Small fart.

Ti moment: One second.

Gros boudouf, gros boyo: Big fatso, big belly.

Bousse to liki: Plug your cunt.

Guelard: Crybaby.

Mousse to neznez: Blow your nose.

Caraille chaud: Hot pan.

Bourique: Asshole.

Nee pu manzer: Born to eat.

Debardere lor la rade: Dockhands.

Savate mariposa: Type of sandal.

Gabloo galoupe derriere moi: Police running behind me.

Marchand salete: Garbage collector.

Descende lor pied: Payback time.

Caro canne brilee: Burnt sugar cane.

Ca c ene discussion bien confidential: This is a very private conversation.

Ti aigre doux: "Small sour sweet." A term of endearment.

Sauver cot capav: Save yourself those who can.

Soutireuse: "Indulger," as in one who spoils a child.

Ca betasse: That dumbass.

Quel Tapaze: What a racket.

Comptroller Sakibonsa: Comptroller Man-that's-good.

Poule Bouilli: Boiled chicken, as in the poulterer's naked body's likeness to one.

Get sa faiseur la . . . vantard li voleur: Look at that braggart. If she's not boasting, she's thieving.

Mo pas ouler croire: I don't want to believe it.

Sinon zot pu perdi zot charme: Otherwise they'd lose their charm.

Karro cane prends dife: "Sugar cane field catches fire." In this instance, referring to Sergent's hair loss.

Langet tor ma: Mother's cunt.

Voleur-caveaus: Graverobbers.

Biscuits manioc: Arrowroot biscuits.

Manzerfes: Ass-eater.

Nanier a foutes: Nothing-to-doers.

Diable p marier en bas pied piment: "The devil is getting married beneath a chilli plant." This literal translation refers to both good and bad weather being equally possible, denoting in some cases the proximity of a cyclone or the derangement of Mother Nature's forces.

Ki kote twalet la: Which way is the toilet?

A droite: To the right.

Merde dimoune: Shit of the world.

Ene la trappe sa . . . mouche dans alouda limonade: It's a trap. The immigration police are going to be here like flies on an alouda lemonade!

Aio mama oh, ki lengrenange mo fine tomber: Oh mother, what kind of trouble did I fall into?

Fouille partout de fond . . . zot fine coquin: Dig around everywhere from top to bottom. Check what they've stolen from us.

Coma to capav . . . to propre race: How can you do this to your own race?

Kete: What?

Dans dilo: In water.

Tire kaka mettre pete: "Remove shit and put back a fart." The literal translation is the rough Mauritian equivalent of "swings and roundabouts."

Aka aka boule caca . . . ister TAC: Mauritian counting rhyme, translating to "shit, shit, ball of shit, worms, worms, ensnared, now, now tack (sounding of a trap)," but carrying the connotation of "you will never catch me."

Acknowledgments

I would be remiss if I did not draw attention to the influence and contributions of the following individuals.

THANK YOU – Ah-Peng (le Boudouf)
Dane Boaz
Nadia Bozak
Ulysses Castellanos
Cécile
John Goldbach
Grace
Inaam Haq
Helen
Lee Henderson
Christopher Heron
Katrina Lagacé
Elysse Leonard
Jeff MacNab
Sherita MacNab
George Mantzios
Behzad Molavi
Monique
Martin Zeilinger

Jay MillAr
Hazel Millar
Rick Meier
Ruth Zuchter
BookThug

and most of all,
Malcolm Sutton, for keeping the faith

Colophon

Distributed in Canada by the Literary Press Group:
www.lpg.ca

Distributed in the United States by Small Press Distribution:
www.spdbooks.org

Shop online at www.bookthug.ca

Edited for the press by Malcolm Sutton
Copy edited by Ruth Zuchter
Designed by Malcolm Sutton
Typeset in Portrait Text

BOOK
PRODUCTION
WAR ECONOMY
STANDARD

Listen to "Dire moi ene coup" at **soundcloud.com/blackderwish**